I.S. 61 Library

W9-BFI-987

I.S. 61 Library

I.S. 61 Library

THEO

THEO

BARBARA HARRISON

Clarion Books ⊙ New York

Clarion Books
a Houghton Mifflin Company imprint
215 Park Avenue South, New York, NY 10003
Copyright © 1999 by Barbara Harrison

The text for this book was set in 14-point Apollo MT.

All rights reserved.

For information about permission to reproduce selections from this book,
write to Permissions, Houghton Mifflin Company, 215 Park Avenue South,
New York, NY 10003.

Printed in the USA.

Library of Congress Cataloging-in-Publication Data
Harrison, Barbara, 1936–
Theo / Barbara Harrison.
p.   cm.
Summary: A twelve-year-old puppeteer performs bravely on and off the stage
after joining the Greek resistance movement during World War II.
ISBN 0-899-19959-3
1. World War, 1939–1945—Underground movements—Greece—Juvenile
fiction. 2. Greece—History—Occupation, 1941–1944—Juvenile fiction.
[1. World War, 1939–1945—Underground movements—Greece—Fiction.
2. Greece—History—Occupation, 1941–1944—Fiction. 3. Orphans—Fiction.
4. Puppet theater—Fiction.] I. Title.
PZ7.H2465Th   1999
[Fic]—dc21
98-45823
CIP
AC

QUM   10   9   8   7   6   5   4   3   2

In loving memory of my parents, Edna (Vlachos) and Frank Harrison, with gratitude for a childhood home alive with people and books, the scent of lamb roasting, the sound of music, laughter, voices chattering into the night

and for my brother, Bill, and my sister, Kay, who are carrying forth virtues learned those many years ago: *arete, philoxenia, sophrosyne,* and *agape*

ACKNOWLEDGMENTS

I drew both inspiration and information from many books and people. The books include *The World of Karagiozis* by A. Yayannos and others; *Karagiozis: Culture and Comedy in Greek Puppet Theater* by Linda S. Myrsiades and Kostas Myrsiades; Errikos Sevillias's *Athens-Auschwitz*, translated by Nikos Stavroulakis of the Jewish Museum in Athens; Margaret Alexiou's *Ritual Lament in Greek Tradition*; and Diane Tong's *Gypsy Folktales*, from which I adapted the story "Yannakis the Fearless." I would like to thank the consistently helpful staffs at Harvard University's Widener Library in Cambridge and at the Gennadeion Library in Athens.

In my travels in Greece, family and friends have been enormously generous. Yioryia Haralambopoulou, in particular, has shared both her home and her experiences growing up in Athens during World War II. Thanks, too, to Lakis and Maria Haralambopoulos for their warmth and hospitality, and to Mark Gregoropoulos, who introduced me to Greece's Gypsy community. I am grateful to Panos Haralambopoulos; and to Babis, Toula, and Takis

Dracopoulos, who, before they died, taught me a great deal about the history, culture, and politics of their beloved country and about the suffering and bravery of the Greek people during World War II. Panos, Babis, and Takis also recounted childhood experiences in Isari, the Arcadian village of their birth.

My deepest appreciation and gratitude to my editor, Virginia Buckley, whose insight, encouragement, and wisdom mean more than I can say.

There's an old story that when God created
the world he had a sieveful of rocks left over.
He threw them over his shoulder and thus
made Greece. On some mountain slopes no
more than a thin veneer of soil exists, or an
occasional crevice in which the village farmer
rushes to plant an olive tree. Only the deep
roots of the olive, the scrub oak, the grapevine
take hold. They are hardy and stubborn,
like the deep roots of the people.

 ONE

In the old neighborhood of Plaka, which lay at the foothills of the Acropolis, Theo stood amidst a crowd of children. The scorching sun was a white-faced hornet in the summer sky. Theo, like the others, was ragged and thin, an emaciated bird. Standing in the shade cast by one of the dusty locust trees bounding the town square, the children were watching an enemy soldier juggle oranges.

The shops facing the square were boarded up: the café, the sweetshop, the butcher. The kiosk, too, was abandoned. Before the war, it had teemed with newspapers and magazines and sundries of every kind: candy, chewing gum, cigarettes, even sponges from the sea and souvenir statues of ancient gods. But now, there was little to sell, and shopkeepers had joined the resistance.

It was not the shiny black boots that attracted Theo, or the irony of an enemy soldier juggling oranges in the midst of famine and war, but the fresh scent of the oranges, made even stronger by nicks in the fruit caused by the juggler's nails.

Theo stood like a sentinel, anticipating a mistake. And when it happened, when the soldier dropped an orange, Theo raced for it, grabbed it, and flew through the cobblestone streets and crooked pathways that stretched like slender fingers out from the square. As the soldier chased in furious pursuit, the other children scattered.

At first Theo heard footsteps behind him, but he did not look back and the sound faded away. He crouched in a recess under a balcony, beads of sweat pouring down his face, trying to catch his breath. No cracked skull, no broken bones, he thought, worried at what might have happened had he been caught.

He almost felt sorry for the soldier. He could sense his surprise and humiliation, but he gloated over the prize in his hands. He made the sign of the cross and heaved a sigh of relief. He'd like to have seen the look on that kraut's face, and he bit deeply into the succulent fruit at the thought.

Theo no sooner savored the taste than he began to shake and tremble. It upset him terribly at these moments, when he became all wobbly and afraid.

His shirt was sopping wet, and his tawny hair darkened by perspiration. Hunger, too, was taking its toll.

He was a short, tough reed with a slight bend in his shoulders. He was thin from hunger and frail looking, yet his hands and feet were extraordinarily large, like a bear cub's, and out of proportion to his body. His features were elongated; his head was the shape of a triangle, like Perseus radiating in the night sky.

Theo left his hiding place through a narrow street leading to the puppet theater where he had performed with his godfather. It was boarded up, but he stood on a stone and peered through an opening near the top of the gate into a small courtyard, eerily silent; his godfather was off to war. The only sound was the chatter of a cricket in the yellow gorse that proliferated in the yard.

In the cluttered workroom of the puppeteer, where he lived with his older brother, Socrates, Theo splashed his face with water and emptied his pockets of potato peel and a hard crust of bread. He sliced the rest of the orange in half and placed it, rind and meat, on a plate in the center of the wooden table.

Shadow puppets hung from dowels in the walls.

The slightest breeze caught a leg or an arm, causing the rustling sound of paper and the flapping of leather. In a corner of the room, sheets for the puppeteer's screen were folded neatly and piled high. Props and discarded light bulbs sat in boxes stacked carefully under the table.

The whining of the puppeteer's cat distracted Theo, and he broke the crust of bread in half, soaked it in water, and fed it to the animal. He noticed the cat's ribs were protruding. If Theo did not say a thing out loud, it did not seem so bad. But today when he saw the cat's deteriorating condition, he couldn't help remarking, "The cat is starving." He fed it the rest of the bread.

Theo walked over to the puppet that his godfather had given him as payment for assisting him with his shows. "You will make a master puppeteer," the man had said to the boy. Theo had beamed with pride. Was not his godfather the most skilled Karagiozis player in all of Greece?

Theo lifted the puppet from the peg. The puppet's potato-shaped head was drawn in profile so only one eye, black as an olive, was visible. His broad, fleshy nose turned under at the end like a beak. He was hatless and barefoot. One arm was conspicuously longer than the other, and a rounded hummock rose on his back. The puppet was made of ox-hide leather.

Two wavy furrows defined his spacious brow. His head was capped with a low patch of black hair and a flourish of sideburns. Painted above his full lips was a thin mustache.

Karagiozis's body was rendered almost in full view. He wore a short jacket open in the front and pantaloons gathered in above the knees. Both jacket and trousers were patched and sewn and tinted red, yellow, and green. At his waist he wore a flamboyant sash with a fringed tassel.

Theo was surprised at the words he made the puppet say—"I'm starving." Even though Theo said them, these were really Karagiozis's words. But, of course, Theo could not deny that he was the one who had said them.

 TWO

Mountains surround Athens, forming a natural amphitheater. The stage itself, the theater proper, gives rise to six hills: the Acropolis, with the Parthenon perched on its peak, the hill of the Pnyx, the hill called Areopagus, the hill of Nymphs, the hill called Mouseion, and the hill of Lycabettos, the highest of the hills. Each day the sun floods the promontories with light.

Like the city, Theo had been shaped by circumstance and time. His mother had died only hours after he was born, and his father had been one of the first victims of the war.

At birth, Theo was such a tiny, scrawny, barely breathing thing that tears formed in his father's eyes. "I will lose the baby, too," he cried. Theo's father vowed to Saint Zacharias, his namesake, that if Theo was saved, he would visit the saint's miracle-working bones in the village of Vasilaki each year on the saint's holy day. Zacharias Alexandros kept his promise until he died.

Only the eagle has the capacity to swallow a snake, but if there had been a snake, Theo would have devoured it. For now he was forced to content himself with the memory of food: the scent of freshly baked bread, the savory taste of salted meat, the soothing texture of rice pudding.

Theo admired the orange on the table. Would Soc think it was a prize? he wondered. He turned to his puppet, "Hey, Karagiozis, little old fellow." He brushed dust off the puppet's bald, furrowed forehead as if he were brushing beads of sweat from his own brow. "Phew!" he said. "That was a close call."

"You can carry this hero stuff too far," Theo made Karagiozis say.

"But I want Soc to be proud of me," Theo answered. "I want so much to be brave in his eyes."

"Brave, ha!" the puppet said. "You're ten years old without a whisker in sight and you shake and tremble. You don't even know what a hero is!"

Theo slapped Karagiozis back on his peg and headed for the streets again in search of food. Of course he knew what a hero was. Hercules, Achilles, Alexander the Great—these were heroes.

Had he not grown up with stories about them? His brother, Soc, too, was a hero. To insure his brother's praise, Theo would set for himself a feat greater than stealing an orange.

But no sooner had he pulled the door shut and turned the corner than he saw Soc approaching.

"*Yiassou*, Theo," Soc called out. As they entered the puppeteer's workroom, Soc clapped his brother's palm with his own and smiled at the earnest face turned toward him.

Soc was tall, powerfully built, with sandy hair, black eyes, and full lips. He appeared older and wiser than his sixteen years. The plump orange failed to capture his attention.

"The Nazis have posted a new edict," Soc said. His face was tense, his tone urgent. "Orphans will be rounded up and sent to Germany." Soc handed Theo the poster he had pulled off a store window.

ATHENS No. 263819

REGISTRATION OF ORPHANS
AUGUST 10, 1943

REGISTRATION OF ORPHANS WILL BEGIN IMMEDIATELY.

CHILDREN BETWEEN THE AGES OF TEN AND SIXTEEN

WITHOUT PARENTS OR LEGAL GUARDIANS MUST REGISTER AT

THE NEAREST GERMAN HEADQUARTERS. ORPHANS WILL BE SENT TO GERMANY TO SERVE ADOLF HITLER, FÜHRER AND REICH CHANCELLOR, ON FARMS AND IN WAR FACTORIES. THOSE WHO DO NOT VOLUNTARILY REGISTER WILL BE ROUNDED UP BY MILITARY PERSONNEL. NECESSARY MEASURES WILL BE TAKEN TO INSURE THAT THIS EDICT IS OBEYED.

HEIL HITLER!
SIGNED,
COMMANDANT, ATHENS

"We will need to leave Athens," Soc said.

Startled by the news, Theo looked around the room as if seeing it for the first time. His eyes focused on the cat. What would become of him? "But where will we go?" he asked.

"To the village of Vasilaki," Soc said.

Theo turned toward his puppet. How could he survive without Karagiozis? Without his props and equipment? What would happen to Karagiozis, as dear to him as a brother? Tears welled in Theo's eyes.

Sensing Theo's anxiety, Soc said, "We'll be safe in the village of Vasilaki. We can be useful to Patir Alex and Kyria Maria, and there's more food in the mountains."

Soc tossed the sack he was carrying to Theo, who opened it quickly. Soldiers' work shoes, in better shape than the sandals he was wearing. The shoes were brown, thick soled, and well crafted. Theo tried them on.

Soc noticed the orange. "A gift from the gods," he said. "Brave little guy! You've done it again." Theo flushed with his brother's praise.

 THREE

At an early age, Theo had revealed an uncanny ability to place himself in someone else's shoes. He thought everyone possessed this ability. He became his soldier father, who was shot dead in the war. He had never known his mother, but in his mind's eye he could see her. It was as if he were his mother.

It was a gift and a burden, this ability to be another person and still be himself. It forced him to dig in just under the sand to avoid being burned by the sun. He lived his life that way—digging in, resurfacing, digging in, resurfacing. He had a disarming smile that came from some rivulet of sadness, some deep sea of memory.

People say you cannot miss someone you never knew, but Theo longed for his mother. "My mother calls to me," he said each time he heard the plaintive song of the wild dove.

Although he knew several people who were in heaven with Christ and the Virgin, he didn't really think death could happen to him. Yet his brother's life and his own were fraught with peril. Theo and Soc were being trained in the dangerous tasks of disrupting power lines and stealing copper wires for use in homemade radio sets. Members of the youth resistance, they were working against the Germans, Italians, and Bulgarians who had plunged Greece into wretchedness.

Theo was good at drawing detailed maps to scale. Both boys knew conventional map signs for roads, bridges, railways, dwellings, mountain ranges, villages, and telegraph and telephone lines. They knew military symbols indicating enemy observation posts, roadblocks, machine guns, trenches and dugouts, tank traps, and artillery units.

They were also adept at identifying the landscape on grid maps: ravines, cuts, culverts, rock clefts, caves, bluffs, gorges, clearings, deep descents, and hairpin bends.

Soc spread out an unmarked map on the table. Three university friends, all resistance fighters, had joined Soc to track the precipitous route from Athens to Patir Alex's village of Vasilaki in the mountains near Delphi. The brothers knew the village because of their father's pilgrimages. But it was not only Saint Zacharias's miracle-working bones that compelled Soc in Patir Alex's direction.

Patir Alex and his wife, Kyria Maria, appeared to live a quiet life in the remote village, but beneath their outward crust, Patir Alex and Kyria Maria were cogs in Operation Elijah, the partisan effort to assist Jewish families fleeing Athens. Operation Elijah activists traced escape routes to mountain villages and out of the country; they identified families who would provide refuge; they issued fake identity cards and baptismal certificates and escorted people to safety.

Theo paid attention for a while, but as the resistance party sketched the route, his mind drifted to the night when paint buckets had crowded the floor of the puppeteer's dwelling as young resistance fighters prepared an attack of graffiti on downtown Athens. At his side was his friend David, Rabbi Elias's youngest child and only son. Their aim: to paint the three-letter word *OXI*, meaning *no,* on buildings and walls.

They followed the grand boulevards alongside the city's central gardens bursting with oleanders and cypresses—Avenue Olga, Avenue Queen Amalia, Avenue Herodou Attikou.

The three letters—*O* (omicron), *X* (chi), and *I*

(iota)—were more than ciphers on the page. Scrawled across buildings and walls, they became resistance fighters in their own right. *OXI* to the Italians, *OXI* to the Bulgarians, *OXI* to the Germans. *OXI* to Il Duce's eight million bayonets, *OXI* to the Führer's screeching airplanes.

In his mind's eye, Theo saw David's feet skimming across pavement, footsteps echoing in the night, feet faster than rumor flying from tongue to tongue. The broad arc of an arm forming a circle. Two crossbars for the *X,* one stalwart column for the *I.* Paint like blood dripping on shoes and feet and pavement. The slosh of the brush against stone and marble and wood. *OXI.*

At Friday night services with the Elias family, Theo learned the rabbi's chants and prayers. At the end of the sabbath evening, Mrs. Elias faithfully placed in Theo's hands a small sack of potatoes, a wedge of cheese, an egg. *Baruch atah, Adonai*—Praised be the Lord—he found himself reciting at odd times of the day and night.

"Perhaps Rabbi and Mrs. Elias will adopt us," Theo said to Soc. It seemed safer to stay in Athens than to leave.

"There's no knowing whether it's a greater risk to be an orphan or a Jew," Soc responded.

Theo chilled at the words. Rumors about the fate of Salonika's Jews had reached Athens. Images stole across Theo's mind: the flash of an *O* for Orphan (like the *J* for Jew) sewn onto Theo's jacket; words Theo could not understand—Buchenwald, Treblinka, Auschwitz—rumors no one chose to believe.

While Soc and the university students traced the route, Theo set up his makeshift puppet stage. It was one meter high and two meters wide. He set the stage on a table, giving it additional height, and arranged three small light bulbs to illuminate the white cloth screen. He masked the lights to give the effect of night. To create the moon, he used an open-ended can covered by translucent orange paper. Theo had meticulously drawn scenery—a high mountain with columns rising on top represented the Parthenon. He had cut out and stapled the scenery to the screen.

Theo pulled puppets from their pegs. His god-father had taught him several stories that had been passed down by word of mouth. But tonight, Theo would perform a play he had written himself based on an incident that took place early in the war. He had never performed the play before, and he approached the job with eagerness.

Theo sounded a cloth-tipped mallet against a

metal gong to herald the opening of the show. The sound was a signal to his brother. Soc winked at the students and scrambled behind the screen. The tension of working on the map vanished as the young resistance fighters gathered in front of the puppet stage.

As the workroom lights were dimmed, leaving only the stage lights, the students applauded the dramatic effect of the moon casting a red glow on the Acropolis. "Bravo," Soc whispered to Theo, at the sound of clapping.

"Welcome, honorable gentlemen and ladies," Theo made Karagiozis say, signaling that the performance was about to begin. "Tonight our theater will present for the first time 'Karagiozis, Brave Soldier.'"

Catcalls and sneers piped from the audience. "Karagiozis, *brave*?" they clamored.

"You'll eat those words, you peasants," Karagiozis said. "Ooooh, I'm hungry," he yelped. "Maybe *I'll* eat them."

From behind the screen, Theo manipulated Karagiozis with a long stick so that the audience could see only the puppet's shadow through the white cloth. He moved Karagiozis's legs so that they appeared to start climbing up the mountainside. It was clearly visible to the audience that Karagiozis, as usual, wore no shoes.

Karagiozis, humpbacked and barefoot, began to climb the steep, winding pathway to the Acropolis. As one foot followed the other, Theo dropped the puppet's head and lifted it, dropped it and lifted it, giving the impression that Karagiozis was winded and gasping for breath.

"Woe is me, woe is me," Karagiozis said. "A man can't even enjoy an evening at home with his family because of this cursed war!"

At the Acropolis gateway, Karagiozis had a clear view of the flagpole on the south side of the Parthenon, where a Nazi flag, a red banner dominated by a black swastika, fluttered in the evening breeze. Soc energetically fanned the flag with one hand, while in his other hand he held the stick attached to the Nazi sentryman guarding the flagpole. Theo and Soc were far enough from the screen so that their shadows could not be seen.

Karagiozis leaned against a broken column as if to recover from the steep climb. Theo raised and lowered Karagiozis's head, this time giving the impression that the puppet was stealing glances at the flagpole. Karagiozis grunted and chattered quietly. "How cruel, how shameless, how outrageous," he said. "A German swastika flying on the Acropolis."

Theo had created the enemy soldier much taller than Karagiozis. He wore stiff, pointed boots and looked far better fed than Karagiozis.

As he watched the gray-green giant strut back and forth with a rifle resting on his shoulder, Karagiozis said, "Eh, what's an old flag, anyway? A piece of cloth. A dust mop." He turned his back on the flag and started to retreat down the hill.

"Hey, Karagiozis!" one in the audience called out. "You can do it!" everyone shouted.

As if hearing the voices, Karagiozis spun in the direction of the flagpole and walked toward the Nazi sentryman.

"I'll break him in two," Karagiozis muttered. "I'll wallop him black and blue." The audience laughed. "But nobody's here to help me . . . Yoo-hoo, Athena, are you there?"

Theo pulled Karagiozis's head toward the sky. Karagiozis hesitated, again frozen by fear, but suddenly he charged toward the Nazi soldier.

The cheering students watched Karagiozis knock the giant to the ground, tear down the swastika from the flagpole, and hoist up the flag of Greece.

Theo's voice came alive with the nasal twang of his trickster puppet as it rang out like a weapon.

"OXI," he exclaimed, his voice bold, persuasive, fiery with passion. *"OXI."*

At that moment Theo was Karagiozis. He could rip the swastika out as neatly as he swiped that orange. And who could stop him?

 FOUR

Theo packed his haversack carefully. He put in a small pocketknife, a map, a compass, matches and candles, two metal spoons, cups, plates, a leather-bound book prized by his father titled *Greek Philosophers,* and his puppet notebooks—small spiral-bound books in which he kept ideas for his shows. He wrapped the photograph of his mother and the icon of the Virgin.

He placed around his neck his christening cross, given to him by the puppeteer. On the chain, too, was a small charm to ward off the evil eye. After he hooked the clasp, Theo brought the cross to his lips, kissed it, and made the sign of the cross. "May the puppeteer be safe," he prayed.

Theo tried to figure out a way to carry Karagiozis so as not to damage any of his parts. He would take one sheet that he could use for a puppet screen.

His brother filled his haversack with candles,

matches, crimpers, fuses, blasting caps, a small amount of a carefully wrapped pliable explosive, paper, and pencils. He also stashed a bundle of letters to Barba. The letters were first drafts. He had already mailed copies in his best handwriting.

Although they were headed for the village of Vasilaki, Theo and Soc dreamed of eventually joining their uncle Aristoteles Alexandros in the United States. They called him Barba, meaning uncle. Soc wrote letters to Barba, even now in wartime when he could not be sure the letters reached him. He posted them to 41–16 47th Avenue, Sunnyside, Queens, Long Island, New York.

A package for Patir Alex and Kyria Maria contained parts for their printing machine and copper wire for the wireless radio. On the package, printed in small neat letters, was their name and address, Patir Alex and Kyria Maria Haralambos. Both boys carried flasks of water.

Theo was determined to take the cat. "The meowing could be a problem," said Soc. "And another mouth to feed. The cat could place us in danger." Theo was annoyed with Soc, always so reasonable, so grown up. Theo's friend David promised that he would watch out for the cat and the puppeteer's house, too. Theo was jealous that

David got the cat. Still, he thanked David for his kindness.

Rabbi Elias placed a gold coin in Theo's hands. "In case of need," he said. He also gave him a small cache of food.

The night before leaving Athens, Theo carried to bed an armful of puppet show paraphernalia: posters, announcements, advertisements, scenes. He scrutinized each item, memorizing favorite designs and ideas.

One item in particular captured his attention. On a poster printed in elaborate capital letters was the puppeteer's name, BABIS GRIGORIS. The handsomely drawn letters were embellished with the tiny figure of Karagiozis depicted in miniature. He was swinging from the crossbar of the *A*, leaning against the column of an *I*, and lounging in the bowl of a *B*.

The ornately crafted letters triggered the memory of his godfather in Theo's mind: his shaggy mustache, the knobby hands, his playful voice. In one instant, he could bray like a donkey; in another, coo like a bird. Theo bit his lip wistfully.

"*Opa,* Theo," Soc blurted out, noticing his brother's brooding expression. He snapped his thumb against his middle finger and pirouetted into the air. "At this very hour Godfather Babis is dancing arm in arm with resistance fighters in the mountains. *Opa!*" Soc said louder, yanking Theo out of bed.

Soc laughed as Theo scrambled to right himself, and arms around each other's shoulders, they leapt across the room, first one foot flying into the air and then the other until the world turned golden beneath their feet. Without undressing, Theo put his head on the pillow and drifted into a sound sleep.

One by one, Soc lifted the treasures that covered Theo like a shield and packed them neatly in a trunk under the puppeteer's bed. In truth, no one knew the puppeteer's whereabouts. Theo and Soc had heard rumors that he had been arrested for resistance activities, interrogated, and imprisoned.

Soc took down from the wall the oath of the ancient healer Hippocrates, which he almost knew by heart. He folded and tucked it in his haversack on top of the bundle of letters and went to bed. The faint ripple of a breeze came through the open shutters.

Soc jolted awake several times, anticipating that it was the hour to leave. Finally, a persistent rapping at the door alerted him. He looked at the clock: 3:00 A.M. "Quickly," he called out to Theo, shaking him. "It's the courier Zappas."

Before the war Zappas hawked plump bread rings covered with toasted sesame seeds piled high on a tray carried precariously on his shoulder. Theo expected Zappas to holler the familiar street cry, "*Koulouria!*" but he was empty-handed, and he only whispered "Hurry, boys" and nodded in the direction of the truck.

With a pang of regret, Theo glanced at the puppets he was leaving behind. Megas Alexandros wore a plumed helmet and carried a sword, and Barba Yiorgos, a shepherd holding a shepherd's crook, was dressed in the pleated skirt of the freedom fighter of the past. "I'll be back for you," he whispered.

Zappas took them to a point fifty kilometers outside of Athens, where they began the trek by foot to Patir Alex's miracle-working village. The sun had not yet made its appearance in the predawn sky. A feeble breeze brushed their faces in the quiet light of the waning moon.

They exchanged farewells. "*Zito* Hellas," Zappas said. Long live Greece. "*Zito,*" the boys responded. May it live long.

Theo adjusted the pack on his back, looked down at his new soldiers' shoes, and called out to them. "Well, let's see what you can do, *pallikaria,*" he said. The pathway was fledged with maquis and tangled scrub oak. It was like a slithering snake, all bends and angles and curves.

At first the trail seemed easy, but soon the earth became rough and broken, and not even a small breeze broke the stifling haze of heat. Paths rose and descended steeply. It was a place of landslides and rock fragments and daunting precipices, where one could easily lose one's way.

They made an effort to avoid well-traveled roads. Fields once inhabited by mice were now crowded with enemy soldiers. They sought out the most difficult tracks, narrow mountain paths fit only for pack animals.

As the sun stole silently across the sky, Theo and Soc stopped every few kilometers. Soc jotted down notes on his grid: "Road begins to ascend, rough wooded slope, altitude 100 meters." Each square on the grid represented one thousand meters.

In the late afternoon, Theo dug for roots and wild green nettles. They paused in the cool shadow cast by a rock, ate sparingly, and rested. Feeling refreshed, they started on their journey again, hoping to make headway before the onset of night.

But no sooner had they turned a sharp bend than they were startled by the irritated barking of dogs. Birds stirred and flew away, dung beetles whirred their wings, and wild bees found safety in clefts in nearby rocks. The sight of the special German convoy with heavy weapons, tanks, and a pack of enormous dogs rattled the boys' bones and sent them for cover.

Dogs, all spittle and snarls, skittish and salivating, strained against leashes held by German soldiers. Theo and Soc leapt like foxes onto stone walls to shake the scent, fled zigzag in one direction, abruptly shifting to another to get them off the track. Buckthorn and broom slapped Theo's face and rocks jutted to break the momentum of his run. A shift in the direction of the wind sent the hounds skittering and frustrated.

Theo got down on his knees, uttered a prayer of thanks to the Lord, and made the sign of the cross.

When the boys found an abandoned sheepfold in which to spend the night, Theo, trembling, pulled Karagiozis out of his knapsack to check that his parts were intact. "Hey, you, little old fellow," he said, counting Karagiozis's fingers and toes.

"It will take a lot more than five hundred fire-breathing dragons to threaten Karagiozis," the puppet said.

In the dark of night, Theo pulled out his leather-bound *Greek Philosophers*. As Soc read, Theo caught echoes of his father's voice. "Those who know the good choose the good," he heard his father say. What did it mean to be good? Theo wondered. "Poor father," Theo wept, "brought down on Mount Elvasan, the Mountain of Wolves, by dumb macaroni eaters."

That night Theo slept with his arm around Soc, behind a bundle of brushwood thick with dry mud.

 FIVE

As the days wore on, Theo began to feel cheated and agitated. His joints were all stiff and ached from the hard ground, and his belly cried out with hunger. Still he and Soc continued their trek, scribbling on paper every hillock, bramble, or potential shelter. He wanted to be with his puppets in the puppeteer's workroom, cutting puppet figures, drawing scenes, creating special effects for his performances. But now he was stuck drawing pathways and bushes.

Early one evening, Soc raided the field of a farmer who kept a few chickens. In the distance, they heard a woman's voice. "Pe-tros," she called out, as if beckoning someone home for supper.

At the sound of the voice, Theo's mother entered his thoughts. Mother, he shouted, as he rushed into her arms. She comforted him with hugs and kisses.

Soc's voice broke his reverie. "Hey, Theo, we've

got a chicken for supper." Theo couldn't believe his ears. A chicken! His mouth watered at the sound of the word. He bustled for kindling while Soc twisted the chicken's neck to kill it. Soc plucked it clean, impaled it on a hardwood stick, and cooked it over a small fire. The meat was succulent. He boiled its bones for broth.

"We must pay the farmer back as soon as possible," Soc said. "It's a debt we cannot forget."

"Indeed," Theo answered, savoring the broth's scent. "May his fields be blessed."

Theo helped himself to water from the farmer's well, carefully lowering the bucket and bringing it up again. Soc heated the water and the boys bathed.

Theo collected brush and covered it with the cloth for his puppet show to try to make a more comfortable bed. As he lay down on the puppet screen, he spoke to Karagiozis, "Hey, little fellow, things are looking up." But before he could even muster an answer, Theo fell fast asleep.

The following day, the brothers started out in the predawn hours determined to make strides before the raging sun seared their skin.

In a corn-rubble field, as Soc paused to jot map signs in his notebook, Theo walked toward a scarecrow, thinking he could make use of some part of it for his puppet show. The day was windless and fiercely hot even in the semidarkness.

As Theo approached the scarecrow, he caught the scent of something rank and sour and noticed a swarm of flies buzzing around the scarecrow's shredded hat. He stopped abruptly, reluctant to go forward, but he was drawn toward it.

As he came closer, he made out the head of a dark-haired woman. She was held fast to a frame with rope supports at the jaw, wrists, chest, and waist, giving the impression of a crucified Christ. A placard around her neck identified her crime. "Killed," it said, "for hiding a British soldier." Maggots invaded her wounds.

Theo retched and vomited until there was nothing left inside him, not even words—only silence, except for the chip, chip, chipping away at the mummified earth to dig a shallow grave. Theo and Soc plodded and scratched, continuing on, all clammy and broken themselves at the sight. They unloosed the woman, pulled away the straw that adhered to her body.

Soc lifted her under the arms, Theo lifted her feet, and they carried her to the hollow. The weight and awkwardness of the body forced them to put it down every few moments, and then to lift it again, put it down, lift it. The tension of their effort was mounting.

The weight of the body shocked Theo. He had nothing to protect his hands from the ice-cold feel of the woman's skin. Was this what *dead* meant? Was this a hero's fate? Her skin was tight and cold even with the sun beating down relentlessly.

"Let's lay the body in the grave with her feet toward the sea," Soc said.

"Toward Mount Olympus," Theo replied. "It's more appropriate for a hero." Soc tugged in one direction and Theo in the other. A burst of nervous laughter edged out of Theo's mouth and then Soc's as the boys realized their predicament. They laid the body down and doubled over in hysterical laughter.

But slowly they lifted the woman again and walked in a half circle around the shallow grave. They placed her feet toward the high mountain so that she would have a full view of Mount Olympus, snow-covered even now in late August.

There was no water to cleanse the body, not even rain—only sweat and salty teardrops. Theo did not say it aloud, but in the recesses of his mind he knew that this could have been his mother, his father, the puppeteer.

Compelled by this idea as much as by any other,

Theo and Soc held a small service. A proper burial was necessary if the victim was to find peace in the other world. People improperly buried would swell up like a blowfish, haunt the living, and never find peace. Their bones would not disintegrate. No solace for the deceased without proper burial. Or for the living.

⊙ ⊙ ⊙

After the scarecrow incident, their luck changed for the good, which Soc interpreted as divine thanks for their act of decency in burying the woman.

The brothers filled the silence of long nights with Karagiozis antics and with passages read aloud from their father's leather-bound book. They sang folk songs of the revolution, popular even now, more than one hundred years after the Greeks had thrown off the yoke of Turkish oppression.

Manamou ta, Manamou ta klephtopoula,
Trone ke tragoudane, olo pinoun ke glendane.

Ma ena mikro, ena mikro klephtopoulo,
Then troi, then tragoudai, ai, then pini, then
glendai.

Mon t'armata, mon t'armata tou kitaze.
Tou, dou fekiou tou lei, Yiassou, Kitso mou,
leventi.

"Mother, dear Mother," Theo and Soc sang out, as if their mother could hear them. "The mountain fighters are singing, feasting, and celebrating; they are festive and triumphant. *Ai,* but, alas, one young patriot seems sad and solitary. *Ai,* he isn't singing or carousing. Haunted by war, he stares at his weapons and calls the rifle at his side by name. *'Yiassou, Kitso mou, leventi,'* he says. Health to you, Kitso, my brave one."

The folk songs were full of truths and half truths, ideas to bolster their sagging spirits; the songs were full of sadness and longing.

Theo practiced skits set at the height of the Greek War of Independence. He reenacted the story of the priest who sang the national anthem as flames engulfed him; and the story of Euphrossini, the Greek heroine, drowned by her husband, Ali Pasha, the Turk, when he discovered her work as a spy.

In his puppet notebook, Theo worked out details of a play about the village of Souli. When the mountain women discovered that Turkish oppressors had massacred their husbands, they formed a circle at cliff's edge and jumped to their deaths, singing:

> A fish cannot live on land,
> Flowers cannot grow on sand,
> Souli women cannot live without liberty.

Within two kilometers of their destination, the brothers were stalking a stray goat when it suddenly dropped from sight. Theo followed it, lowering himself through the bramble of roots and low-lying bushes into a hole in the ground that led into a spacious chamber.

It was much too risky to keep the goat, but the cave could become a refuge.

The floor of the entrance room was smooth and level. Just beyond it there was a sudden drop of two meters and a space in the shape of an ellipse. In this room was a hearth of stone. A mound of ashes, no longer smoldering, provided evidence that the ventilation in the cave was remarkably good.

Passageways linked a cluster of five medium-size rooms. The brothers realized that the cave might come in handy later. In addition, it would give them time to get the maps in shape and prove that, indeed, they were old enough to fend for themselves.

☉ ☉ ☉

For several nights Theo and Soc worked on the maps that would be used by Jews escaping Athens. They singled out shelters, sanctuaries, shortcuts, wells, abandoned sheepfolds—all necessary on any discreet passage from Athens to Vasilaki.

At times, Theo chafed at Soc's efficiency and bossiness. "Scrub behind your ears," Soc said. "We don't want to embarrass ourselves when we arrive in Vasilaki."

Sometimes very late at night when the howling of mountain wolves kept Theo awake, Soc would put his arm around him and tell him stories about America, where Barba waited for them.

Home, Theo realized, had become his brother rather than a physical place. Home was Soc as audience and actor in a puppet show. Or his brother talking about the American game of baseball and the great Joe DiMaggio, or dreaming out loud about studying to be a doctor in the United States.

Theo's fear about being captured and sent with other orphans to Germany began to diminish. Yet, one night when the moon was a mere sliver and only one candle lit the cave, Theo bombarded Soc with questions. "Why are we at war? Why is God so quiet? Who is God? Where is God?"

The candle cast a haunting shadow on the cave wall, and Soc walked toward it, pointing to the shape of an arm beckoning him forward. Soc became animated. "Look," he called out. With his finger, he traced the larger-than-life profile of a forehead, nose, mouth, and beard. He traced the shoulder, arm, hand. "There he is!" he shouted.

The brothers interpreted it as a good sign.

 Six

Yet, in the dark, dark circles of the underworld, helmeted giants clambered upward within reach of Theo and Soc Alexandros.

Theo lit the votive light. "With the Virgin's blessings, we cannot fail," Soc said. There was no hint of fear in his voice. Only the candle flickered. Soc stroked Theo's hair. They embraced, kissed each other on both cheeks, and left the safety of the cave.

Theo and Soc had rehearsed the plan several times. Their aim was to save a barrel of olive oil confiscated by the Nazis for use in Nazi war machines. They had received no orders to perform such a task. They simply had seen the oil and decided it would be a generous gift to Patir Alex and Kyria Maria.

They aimed to save just enough olive oil to take to the village, only what they could carry easily. What a way to announce themselves to Patir Alex and Kyria Maria. Suitable compatriots in the resistance movement!

Soc intended to bore one small hole in the top of the barrel, insert a tube, and let the oil seep undetected through the conduit into a smaller container at the base of a tree, where Theo would monitor the siphon.

What couldn't be saved, they earmarked for Greek soil. Rather than let the enemy use precious Greek olive oil for food or machinery, they would siphon it off into the earth. The brothers were well aware that the Germans called such destruction agricultural sabotage. The penalty was death.

Theo followed the contours of Soc's crouched figure across the grass to the barrel, which rose like a rotund column from the ground, and he observed Soc hoist himself on top of it. He glanced down to check the siphon connected to the container at his feet, then looked back toward Soc.

In what seemed no more than a hair's breadth of time, he noticed agitated motion, the sound of a scuffle. He held on to a low-lying branch of the tree, peering to find his brother's figure in the distance. Where was Soc, that know-it-all? He had disappeared.

Theo strained his ears in the direction of the

enemy camp. He heard the guttural sound of German being spoken, the smack of a rifle butt, insane laughter, and then a tug on the siphon tubing and fast-paced footsteps in his direction.

A high-pitched siren, like the cry of a wolf, sent Theo scrambling for cover. He fled toward the cave and slipped through one of the narrow passageways and crouched in a corner of the room. The votive light had extinguished. With trembling hands, he groped for the matches and lit the candle.

In the flickering gloom of candlelight, he paced back and forth, praying for Soc's return. He prayed to the Virgin. He prayed to Saint Zacharias. He kissed the photograph of his mother. He pulled out his puppet. He could muster no words from Karagiozis. The puppet was silent as the moon.

Theo was not used to being this alone. But there was no choice to behave otherwise, so he bolted toward the barrels and huddled in a forlorn heap behind an ancient olive tree and waited.

At dawn, before the crowing of the first cock, the air was flat and motionless. Theo was alone and trembling.

Afraid to move, he was distracted by a splinter in his finger that he couldn't dislodge. As he shivered in the darkness, his mind darted in and out of memory—the cold, the hunger, the laughter of German soldiers.

In Athens, Nazi soldiers had thrown crusts of bread from the window of a high office building. On the way down, the bread disintegrated into crumbs. The men pointed and laughed as Theo and other children scampered like tiny sparrows pecking about among dead leaves for seeds.

At first, Soc's decision to leave Athens had seemed smart. Not only were Soc and Theo orphans, but city people were eating the meat of horses, donkeys, mules. Garbage trucks were being used to carry the dead. Theo's belly was swollen with hunger. What other choice had they had?

But look what it had come to. Theo turned toward the tread of feet and saw Nazi soldiers marshaling a prisoner. Soc was blindfolded, his hands tied behind his back. Hidden by high parched grasses, Theo crept alongside them as they walked in the direction of an open space—where they stopped.

At the click of guns, Theo turned toward the Nazi soldiers aiming point-blank at their prisoner.

As he faced the firing squad, Soc tossed back his head and shouted, as if he knew his brother could somehow hear, "Hey, little fellow, don't forget to pay Petros for the chicken we owe him." Then he started to sing out words from the ballad, *"Manamou ta, Manamou ta klephtopoula."*

⊙ ⊙ ⊙

The crack of gunfire awakened the old priest. He sat bolt upright on the side of his bed rubbing his eyes. Next to him his wife also stirred. His tongue was thick from the wine he had drunk the night before. Patir Alex tried to recall what day it was and remembered that this was September 1, the Day of the Writer of the Book of Fate. On this day the Angel of Death scribbled names of those who would die in the coming year.

Quickly he put on his trousers and threw his cassock over his head. He glanced at his wife. He was agile for a man his age. "May your eyes be fourteen," she called out, as he darted out the door, stopping only once to relieve his bladder.

⊙ ⊙ ⊙

Two doors down, the president of the village council nicked his chin with his razor at the rattle of machine guns. The lather on his face disguised an expression of satisfaction.

⊙ ⊙ ⊙

At the crack of the machine guns, Theo Alexandros witnessed Soc pitch forward and fall to the ground. For a second everything was still. Theo remained silent—as if it was just possible the terrible instant could reverse itself. But then a Nazi soldier kicked the lifeless youth. Out of Theo's mouth came an agonized bark, like that of a defenseless animal caught unaware.

Theo bolted toward the scene, recklessly, pounding his fists on the chests of the Nazi soldiers, heaping himself on his brother's body, stretching his arms and legs out on top of him, forming a human shield. But too late.

Dumbfounded, the Nazis plucked him off as if he were a tiny insect. The boy broke loose and started running in the direction of the hills and into the open arms of the approaching priest. At last.

Theo struggled to talk, but he could barely form the words. They were all broken and confused. Patir Alex was able to make his way through them. "Your brother has set out on the road to God," the priest said.

At the place of execution, the Nazi troopers had vanished, leaving the body totally exposed. Huge carrion crows frisked in the dirt next to the body. Theo shooed them away with a motion of his arms.

"The place is called Golgotha, after the site of the Crucifixion," Patir Alex said grimly.

Patir Alex made the sign of the cross, wrapped the young guerrilla fighter in his cassock, and lifted his body over his shoulder. He staggered slightly as he adjusted the weight of the body and started toward the village. Head and arms loosened from the cassock and flapped against his back.

Theo fell behind. All color had drained from his lips. As he stumbled forward, following the trail of blood, he was mumbling something about Petros and chickens.

 SEVEN

The village was a whitecap of sea at the crest of a wave. A cluster of whitewashed houses with orange tile roofs rose in terraces on the mountainside. A narrow path spiraled toward the village square.

For centuries little had changed in the village. Goats still grazed on the mountainside and oxen were trained to the plow. The wine trough for the grapes stood in the churchyard, and a circular stone threshing floor was situated in a nearby field. Twice a year a caravan of Gypsies visited the village with an organ grinder and trained monkeys. The Gypsies sold wares from the outside world.

In a blur of confusion, Theo heard the priest call out to his wife, "Zacharias Alexandros's elder son is dead." Theo lowered his head, the word *dead* echoing in his ears.

From all directions villagers crowded the streets

in a chorus of outrage and lamentation: "These are the dangerous hours, *Lelé, Lelé!* Italians came and then Germans and Bulgarians, *Lelé, Lelé!*"

In a room used for storing goat cheese and olives and on a table used for plucking chickens, Kyria Maria, the priest's wife, washed Soc's body. She tied his jaw and sprinkled him with rose water. From the waist down she wrapped him in a winding sheet. Occasionally her eye glimpsed the flowerpots outside the window and the spider weaving a web in the corner. A comfortless breeze came from the direction of the graveyard.

Theo held a lighted candle in his hand. His eyes were red, swollen, gritty, his lips parched and chapped, his face flushed. His clothes were splattered with blood. Kyria Maria tried to coax the child to rest, but he refused. While his wife worked, Patir Alex made the necessary preparations for the burial service.

Theo watched Kyria Maria fill a tub with water. She instructed him to bathe. A village boy brought him clothes—the only things worth keeping of his own were his trousers, his name Theo Alexandros sewn neatly into the lining, and his soldiers' shoes. "My sympathy to you," Fotis said, handing Theo the clothes.

Theo struggled to talk, but the words were entangled in his mind like the roots of bramble and bunchberry. He couldn't explain what he had seen, and he uttered sounds more like an animal than a boy.

In the churchyard, the priest grasped the thick rope attached to the bell hammer and wrapped it around his wrists and sounded the huge bronze church bell slowly in mourning. Patir Alex was muscular as an ox, although in age he had become somewhat flaccid—still an ox, but an old ox.

"His thread is cut, his spindle wound full," murmured Patir Alex, the words half sung, half spoken as he and Kyria Maria lifted the corpse into the rough-hewn pine box. On his head she placed a crown of white flowers used in the wedding ceremony, as she always did when one died so young and unwed. The earth would be his bride.

She put a coin in his mouth to ferry him across the River Styx. Theo heard the woman call death by name. She called him Charon and chided him for writing the name of this splendid youth in the Book of Fate.

In his right hand Patir Alex held the ornately decorated censer: "O Lord, give him rest in the bosom of Abraham and number him among the just, through His goodness and compassion as our merciful God . . . "

The priest repeated under his breath "among the just" and, through the haze of smoke and incense given off by the censer, looked in the beady, darting eyes of the president of the village council, who was fanning himself with his stiff narrow-brimmed felt hat.

He wore a white linen suit and shiny black patent leather shoes, and he carried a cane with a decorated pommel. He was the only property owner in the village, the only one to place teeth in a glass next to his bed when he went to sleep.

Theo stood next to the priest at the gravesite as the priest poured wine in the form of a cross over Soc's body and recited the final words of the service, "You shall sprinkle me with hyssop and I shall be clean. You shall wash me and I shall be whiter than snow." The congregation joined Patir Alex in singing the hymn of lamentation: *"Eonia, e mnemne,* May his memory be eternal."

Patir Alex motioned Theo to toss a handful of earth into Soc's pinewood casket, signaling the final act of respect. "May God forgive him," the priest chanted.

Theo unfastened the cross from around his neck

and placed it in Soc's casket. He gave the gift spontaneously. The gesture was motivated by his desire to send some part of himself with Soc and to win for his brother a safe journey.

◉ ◉ ◉

Hushed talk at the funeral centered on the courage of the Greeks in pushing the Italians back. "The Virgin is on our side," they reassured one another.

To Theo, the Virgin seemed fast asleep.

In Athens people buried family members in unmarked garden plots in order to use their ration cards rather than officially declare their deaths. The village had already lost ten of its most able men. Another thirty were fighting in the mountains.

That night Kyria Maria kindled a fire to warm the wheat porridge. The twigs crackled loudly, out of proportion to the smallness of the flames—a good omen. The wise woman uncovered the wireless hidden amidst the holy icons. Theo listened as she made contact with Athens and decoded the message they had been waiting for—Operation Elijah had begun.

If things went according to schedule, Rabbi

Reuben Elias, disguised as a Greek Orthodox priest, would soon be arriving in the village of Vasilaki with his son, David. He was the first of the Athens Jews scheduled to be rescued. Under the pretense of taking Rabbi Elias and David to a neighboring village in need of a priest, Patir Alex would escort them to the Convent of the Virgin. There they would meet the Gypsy leader Andonis and travel with him to port.

Theo had been taught not to cry in pain. In fact, when Kyria Maria took the deeply embedded splinter out of his finger, he felt little pain. Yet, alone with the priest and the wise woman, he began to tremble, and tears cascaded down his cheeks.

Patir Alex filled a copper vessel with wine from the barrel and offered it to the boy. Theo took a hefty swallow, then he uttered the first clearly formed words since his brother's execution. With tears streaming down his face, he said, "Thank you for burying my brother." He hesitated for a moment and then asked, "Could I have saved my brother?"

The old priest and his wife exchanged glances. Kyria Maria said quickly and emphatically, "There was nothing you could have done." The votive light flickered in a rose-tinted glass cup and cast a twilight glow in the room. The past was alive in the present, the gods of Homer and Hesiod, the god of Moses and the New Testament apostles. Old gods and new flourished side by side with the living. The priest recited no more than the opening lines of Homer's *Iliad*, and Theo, his heart broken by sorrow, alone in the village except for the priest and the wise woman, fell into a fitful sleep.

 ƎIGHT

The morning after the funeral, the priest greeted the president of the village council at the door. The president's hair was pomaded and scented, and he wore his linen suit and shiny patent leather shoes. In one hand he held his cane with the decorated pommel. In the other he held his narrow-brimmed hat. "I've come for the boy," he said pompously.

"What business is the boy of yours?" asked the priest.

"The German commandant is looking for a courier and personal attendant." The president's onyx ring glistened as he gestured toward Theo, who was picking tiny stones out of the pile of beans on the table. Beads of sweat formed on Theo's forehead. His hands began to tremble.

"The boy stays here," said the priest.

"The commandant would have taken him sooner,

Goatbeard, but the child wears winged sandals. The commandant is prepared to pay for him."

"The boy is not for sale," said the priest.

"Not even for a sack of flour, Goatbeard?"

"The boy is not an article of merchandise."

Theo felt as if his body had lost all sensation.

"Not even for two sacks of flour, Goatbeard? Two sacks of flour would provide enough Communion bread for months." He paused, waiting for the priest's reply.

When none came, he went on, "You are as stubborn as a mule, Alex. Don't you see that we are losing this war, that Greece is . . . "

Abruptly, Kyria Maria entered the room. "The boy is sick," she said. When the president saw the woman, his expression softened. "Look at him, Pino," she said, calling the president by his childhood name.

"It is not only that his belly is bloated and his feet bruised and blistered, but he is feverish and has a strange rash on his stomach and back. I worry," she said, hesitating as she spoke, "that it could be contagious, Pino, something dangerous to the commandant." Her tone was frightened, convincing.

She invited him to observe the boy's rash, but the president of the village council backed toward the door.

"Fool," said the priest as the man left. "Toothless old sardine."

"Sour-faced cuttlefish," added his wife.

◎ ◎ ◎

The summer had been long, hot, and dry. There had been no rain in eighty days. The grapes ripened early on the vine and were covered with a coating of dust.

Black-headed buntings had made a sweep through the vineyards devouring some of the grapes. Patir Alex cursed the birds. He worked the vineyard with George Christos and his son, Fotis, who kept beehives and raised pigeons as a source of food. The beehives were thriving, but raising pigeons had been made difficult by the war.

In the early morning hours the grape pickers greeted each other with nods, fingers to their lips to hush even a whisper. Their hands moved deftly among the clusters. They picked quickly. The grapes were cool and plump in their hands.

Theo pulled off the leftover leaves, and Kyria Maria separated the tiny undersized grapes that she would dry as raisins. To extract the juice, Theo and Patir Alex trampled barefoot on the grapes in wide-rimmed, broad-based barrels. Silence except for the *swish, swish, swish* of bare feet crushing the grapes.

Patir Alex added a portion of resin to the must. As this year's barrels were blessed and prepared to ferment, last year's were opened. But no fanfare accompanied the festivities, no songs. In the vineyard everyone was quiet.

The pruning of the vines would begin in the spring. For now, the villagers offered prayers. They thanked the Virgin for allowing them to finish their task without interruption from Nazi soldiers. They also thanked Dionysus, the wily god of wine.

⊙ ⊙ ⊙

In Theo's heart there were no lines of demarcation, no elusive borders between anger, terror, and despair. Grief found a roothold and dug in deeply.

I'm totally alone, Theo thought. From his deepest self he heard Karagiozis. "Hey, little old fellow. *I'm* here. Look, little fellow."

"The world is over," Theo said to Karagiozis. "If Soc is dead, we must be dead, too."

Each night Theo drenched his pillow with tears, and during the day he cried in his head so that no one could see. In his heart, the desire for revenge grew. Thoughts of anger fermented like yeast.

While kneeling at his brother's grave one morning, in his mind's eye Theo saw Soc standing tall like a cypress tree, his body festooned with poppies and twigs of myrtle. On his head, a ring of delicate white flowers; around his neck, a stethoscope. Soc bent over and listened to the pulse of a severed torso. He connected a finger to a hand, a leg to a trunk. On all fours he searched for a head to match the body, an arm for the torso. Sticking out of Soc's pocket a packet of letters to his uncle in America.

Theo wanted to plunge a dagger into the heart of a Nazi soldier. To acquire a memento—a Nazi bullet, an insignia, identification tags. He longed to bury the prize deep in the ground next to his brother's grave.

In the days following the execution, Theo learned the ways of the villagers. Patir Alex assigned the boy to the church. Theo became the candle maker, toller of the bells, and protector of the icon of the Virgin. In this cool and holy place he companioned the saints, attended to the dust that accumulated on their chins and in their eyes, transforming them into his brother, his mother, his father, living beings in the life of his mind. He occasionally spoke to them. "What in the long run will become of me?" he asked. "I would like you to be proud of me," he said.

Saint Zacharias's miracle-working bones were housed in an ornate bronze container securely placed in a locked glass enclosure in the altar. Theo's father's vow to Saint Zacharias prompted Theo to be especially conscientious about keeping the bronze and glass shining.

Once a week he lifted the bronze box out of the glass and shined it till he could see his own reflection mirrored in the veneer. He would place his ear on the box and listen hard for a few minutes, because it was said that on occasion Saint Zacharias could be heard rustling about.

In the evening Kyria Maria listened regularly to Allied radio news from London, Cairo, Moscow, Athens—whatever station she could get. Despite the passage of time, plaudits continued to pour in for the heroic stand the small Greek nation had made against the Italians. Three years had passed since the Italians attacked Greece on the Greek-Albanian border, but the ultimatum story was told again and again and emboldened the Greeks:

"In the middle of the night, dressed in his night-gown and robe, John Metaxas, the Greek prime minister, opened the door, and ushered the Italian Count Grazzi into his study, where Grazzi handed Metaxas an ultimatum for war—either Greece permit Italian forces to enter the country without incident or Italy would attack.

"The prime minister's answer to the Italian ambassador," said the newscaster, "resounds in the hearts of free people throughout the world. '*OXI*, no, unequivocally no.'"

 Nine

Theo assisted the priest in morning and evening vespers. He joined him on expeditions to neighboring villages. Their most pressing task became the burial of the dead.

The priest found the broken-boned stonemason dumped in a heap in front of the church. The body of the Gypsy bear trainer was discovered floating in the village well. His bear had disappeared.

It soon became clear to Theo that as the priest made his way from village to village, holding services in squares and churches, he observed the activity of the Nazis with the keen eyes of an owl. He was not only an observer. This very week he was scheduled to deposit arms at a convent twenty-five kilometers from the village.

As he swept the altar, Theo was startled by artillery under the altar table. Theo touched the cache of small arms—rifles, machine guns, revolvers. He eyed one in particular, a Nazi Luger, a small pistol, black and shiny and more valuable to him than the most fragrant orange.

As Theo touched the sleek, textured handle and ran his finger across the cylinder, he became consumed by the idea that skillful use of the gun would be the summit of bravery. He became filled with certainty that with this instrument he could prove his mettle.

Yet, as certain as he was, he imagined the shattering sound of gunfire. The memory of human blood and guts appeared before his eyes. The image startled him, and for a second the gun became a force of cowardice, a force of evil. But as his eyes refocused on the gleaming handle, he equated goodness with the gun. He equated God with the gun.

He was attempting to dislodge it when he heard the sound of footsteps. Quickly he pulled the gun from the pile and placed it inside his shirt. It was cold against his skin.

Although impatient to learn the skill of guns and killing, he began to learn from Kyria Maria words to say at crossroads, at wells, at rivers; he learned rituals to ward off the evil eye and the medicinal value of plants and herbs. He learned quickly.

"For a wound, crush the leaves of rosemary or ripplegrass in your palms and apply them," she said. "To stop bleeding, apply direct pressure to the wound with a cloth." The more Theo learned, the more he wanted to know about the art of healing.

Theo harvested the dandelion, the mallow, the stinging nettle. "The leaves of the dandelion can be eaten as lettuce, and the roots roasted and used as coffee," Kyria Maria said. "Starch from the acorn can be used for bread. A good-sized oak yields forty kilos of acorns," she said. "Starch can also be obtained from the asphodel. The long, leathery pods of the carob tree are edible—and the dried fruit of the strawberry tree."

Although the wise woman knew simples and drugs, she was not a practitioner of black magic. Still, many said that she had seen the seventh star, that she had held it in her hands, meaning she was capable of binding and unbinding. She performed many purgings of the body of evil spirits. In short, she was a spiritual as well as a physical healer, and people for kilometers around marveled at her ability.

Theo also learned from the wise woman to gather cicadas. The first cicada that he caught darted from palm to palm in his hands, seeking an exit. In capturing it, he wounded it—a leg came off—and the boy caught sight of the limb out of the corner of his eye.

In a test of grit, Theo plucked the wings of the insects, one by one. They were carried by the wind across the rough, impoverished earth. Theo roasted the bodies and stored them in a deep crevice in a rock. The coolness served as a preservative.

But it was the gun that occupied him.

 T≤N

At midday, when the September sun filled the dome of heaven like a Cyclopean eye, Theo followed a path along the remains of the medieval wall of the city.

Villagers recalled the period long before Patir Alex and Kyria Maria's time when one person after another was brought down by disease. The villagers had dug a furrow and plowed a magic circle around the village. This was to keep away the bad giant who had carried the bubonic plague that wiped out half the population.

Patir Alex defined an imaginary circle within which he determined Theo would be safe. The house was at the very center of a circle that encompassed the well, the cemetery, and nearby fields. Since Theo was an orphan taken in by the village priest and his wife, villagers called him Soul Child.

Theo descended into the familiar hole in the

ground. There, in his cave refuge, he lifted from a corner his worldly possessions. He looked at the icon of the Virgin. On the back of the icon were the names of his parents and grandparents, with their dates of birth and death.

He carefully carved the name of his brother, the date he was born, and the date he died. He then carved his own name and the year he was born. He untied the bundle of letters stored in a paper wrapper, early versions of letters to his uncle that Soc had practiced writing. One by one, he read them.

Dear Barba,

I can't tell you how happy we are to know that you and our aunt are preparing a room for us that overlooks a playground in Sunnyside, Queens. And that you are investigating schools and universities. And that you are happy about my decision to become a doctor. My medical education will require years of study, but I am prepared for the work.

Each day Theo and I study English, and little by little we are able to say, "Hello. How are you? Do you have bread? Water? Food?" Theo talks to his puppet Karagiozis in English. And I have learned the English word for bronchochile—*goiter*—that rascal ailment that plagues our dear aunt. I'm not sure how Mama or Papa would feel, although I suspect they would think it foolish, but Theo wants to be a puppeteer.

Love,
Soc

Dear Barba,

The Germans are doing everything in their power to suppress the news. One newspaper after another is being shut down, but the Greeks prize the printed word as highly as they prize a crust of bread. They have arrested Yiannis for printing a small tabloid and they have arrested his son Stefanos for delivering it. We saw Yiannis after he was released from German headquarters in Halandri. He was limping badly and his face was all bleeding and bruised. Is it true that the Americans are about to enter the war? Tell them to hurry, Barba.

Love,
Soc

Dear Barba,

Theo seems obsessed with bravery. And he keeps pushing me to define it for him as if it were as easy as unscrambling a simple equation. I told him about the two university students who climbed the Acropolis through the southwest entrance, through the great porticoes, past the Temple of Athena Nike, where they snatched the Nazi flag and hoisted the great blue and white. Ah, the danger, the bravery. But is there a cost to courage, and is it worth it?

Love,
Soc

Dear Barba,

A fellow student asked me if I wanted to join the resistance. We talked about Communism and its value in a poor country such as our own. There is little question in my own mind or in Theo's that the sharing of property and wealth protects the poor. There seems to be great value in a political system that promotes sharing over competition and acquisition.

Love,
Soc

Dear Barba,

Theo is the best puppeteer in all of Hellas. He's gifted not only in making the puppets but as an actor. And I must say his shows—with only me as audience (and sometimes actor)—make both of us laugh until we cry. Sometimes there is no one I would rather be with in the whole world than Theo.

Love,
Soc

Theo folded the last letter carefully and tucked it as a talisman in his shirt pocket. He turned toward Karagiozis. The puppet was fifty centimeters high; the leather had been stretched on a wooden frame and meticulously cut and then scraped in places with glass until translucent.

Theo wiped away a tear that fell on the puppet. He lifted the puppet in his hands and spoke to him. "Hey, Karagiozis, little old fellow, Patir Alex tells me that Soc is on the road to God. Oh, dear, what will become of us?"

"Oh, shut up, little brother," he made the puppet answer. "Do something about it. Prove your fiber, your pluck, your fortitude. Become a hero, idiot. Did you pay Petros back for the chicken? Eh? Eh?"

In his knapsack Theo carried the gun. He placed the pistol on the remains of an ancient libation table and stared at it. He followed its outline with his eyes. He picked it up and held it in his hands. He shined the pistol and looked through the sight. He worshiped the gun as if it were a god.

As the boy made his way back, he followed a rustling sound to the crest of a hill and saw in the tangled network of brush a small bird.

I will catch it, he thought, and offer it as a gift to the wise woman and the priest. But as the bird thrashed about, Theo realized that its wing was broken. He held the bird in his hands and examined it as a father might examine a hurt child.

He brought the bird to his cheek. He felt its heartbeat and the warmth of its body. He carried the bird to the house and placed it in a box. In the sides of the box he cut windows. He filled the box with bark, brush, and berries and kept it by his bed.

Gently he brushed the bird's feathers with his forefinger. He built a ladder of twigs on which the bird could stand.

"It'll be okay, little fellow," he said.

⊙ ⊙ ⊙

To Theo, Patir Alex's day had seemed relatively calm—one baptism, one confession, and Papageno's bath. It was the bath that wore Patir Alex out—even with Kyria Maria and Theo's help.

The only person in the village who acted as if there was no war was Papageno, the village simpleton. On his daily peregrinations around the village, he held in his hands an egg-shaped skull that he claimed was Mozart's.

The skull had small eye sockets, a vertical forehead, and jutting cheekbones. At the left temple was a fracture line, which, according to Papageno, was responsible for the headaches that Mozart suffered. Papageno carried his jawless Mozart in two hands lifted in front of his forehead, lurching from side to side down village pathways, singing arias from *The Magic Flute*.

The Germans were entertained by Papageno, and the Greeks took him for granted. About once every three months, the priest and his wife would drag Papageno into the empty church, fill the baptismal font with water, and douse him. They scrubbed Papageno with a brush from head to toe and dressed him in a clean pair of trousers and shirt.

While the baptism took place, Mozart's skull would sit on the altar, much to the priest's distaste, very near Saint Zacharias's bones. Nonetheless Mozart seemed to keep Papageno happy—and although he hated the baths, he thanked Patir Alex and Kyria Maria with their favorite aria, "Papapapapapapapapapapapa . . . "

Although aberrant, Papageno possessed a talent that probably could have taken him to the great opera houses of the world. But strange behavior set in early in Papageno's life—his parrotlike repetition of words, not thank you once, but thankyouthankyouthankyou, in a half stutter, half mumble. Only Mozart arias came out crystal clear.

Everybody in the village knew *The Magic Flute,* and it didn't take long for Theo to begin humming arias. That Mozart died in Vienna, attended at burial by only the gravedigger, was not lost on the Greeks. They forgave the composer for having been born in the country of the Führer.

But several villagers in Vasilaki believed that someone had praised Papageno as a child so lavishly for his promise and talent that he had been given the evil eye. So villagers tried to accompany words of high praise with spitting gently three times to ward off potential evil. *Phtoo. Phtoo. Phtoo.*

Kyria Maria thought that Theo, like Papageno, was light-shadowed, that he had a pure soul and a pure heart, and that he could easily be affected by magic.

She believed that he was in need of powers that she held at her command, the benevolences of wild herbs and plants and skills of binding and unbinding. To protect Theo, Kyria Maria pinned to his undershirt an amulet with a tiny knob of garlic. The wise woman mumbled the *xemetrima* over Theo. She had done the same for Papageno. "Garlic in your eyes," she often said aloud.

Theo accepted the authority of Kyria Maria and felt empowered by the protection.

 ELEVEN

As he approached the hives, Theo could hear the droning of myriad honeybees. Despite the war, the spirit of the beehive remained undaunted—the dancing and swarming, the transformation of nectar into honey, the making of the wax, the tending of the young.

The bees were oblivious to sounds of life and death outside their own natural and profound mysteries. And who would violate the sacred chambers of the hive, the fecundity of the queen, the cells and storehouses of the golden colony?

Fotis, Theo's village friend, handed him a honeycomb. Theo devoured it. "It has been said that when a colony of bees dies of starvation," Fotis explained, "all the bees die at once because they share food with each other unselfishly until not a droplet is left."

Fotis showed Theo the hives and shared his plan

for terrorizing the president of the village council, that notorious collaborator who sold information to the Nazis. Fotis moved closer to Theo, and almost in a whisper, he said, "Stingers are amazing weapons. A swift and forceful sting can cause instant death."

Theo, in sheer admiration, slapped Fotis so hard on the back that the boy practically fell onto one of the hives. Fotis tousled Theo's hair, and they wrestled like bear cubs oblivious to anything except the impressive act of revenge that Fotis had devised.

It never occurred to Theo that the president of the village council could really die—an old wives' tale passed down through the years. But they would put it to the test. A boyish prank. A diversion. Pure hearsay, wish fulfillment.

As they approached the outskirts of the village, they saw three German soldiers talking to great-grandmother Aspasia. They crept close enough to hear.

"Give us your cow or we will dig up your dead husband and boil his bones for soup," they said.

"Can't you see?" she said. "The cow will give birth in a few days." The German soldiers bent over the animal. Pushing its belly, they realized that the old woman's words were true.

"All right, then," they said, "after the calf is born, the mother is ours."

"Poor great-grandmother Aspasia," Fotis whispered. "She takes care of this poor cow as carefully as she tends her pots of basil."

As soon as the Germans left, Theo and Fotis raced to her side. "Don't fret, Kyria Aspasia," Theo said. "Everything will be all right." But, in fact, Theo knew that there was little they could do.

Within a few days the calf was born and the Germans returned for the animal. The old woman begged once again. "Please, the calf will die if his mother is taken from him and he has no milk."

The Germans ignored her pleas. "Use your own teats, Grandmother." They laughed and led the cow away. The calf died shortly afterward.

⊙ ⊙ ⊙

It was not long after that a swarm of bees invaded the president's house. The bees attacked the president of the village council in bed, landing on his head as if he were a sweet-smelling flower. He shooed them away with his arms, and then he started to swat them as they engulfed his arms and legs as if he were goldenrod or clover.

When he started to swat, they began to sting and he began to panic. He ran out the door through the village like a man with Saint Vitus' dance. He was stark naked and barefoot, without his shiny black shoes, his narrow-brimmed hat, and his cane with its decorated pommel. His teeth were still in the glass by his bed.

His arms flailed. Swatting first here and then there, he was all elbows and knees. The cruel and wicked man spent the next days in bed covered with poultices of crushed raw onions alternating with the milk of the dandelion root. He was unaware that a mouse had gnawed a hole in his flour sack.

Flour spilled out over the wooden planks like a thick blanket of snow. He missed several of the autumn holy days.

Theo and Fotis held an emergency meeting. "He could really die," Theo said, truly realizing for the first time the lethal power of the bee sting. "May the Lord forgive us," he added.

"The old quisling deserves it," Fotis said.

"Spineless prickly pear," Theo added, unable to admit to the twinge of guilt that he had caused pain to another human being. Was causing pain what heroism was all about?

 TWELVE

His trust in Patir Alex grew, and Theo led the priest along a stony path to the cave. The entranceway to the cave was still camouflaged by low-lying mallow and tangled vines. Theo lowered himself through the bramble of roots and grasses and reached upward to watch Patir Alex awkwardly make his way through the cave opening. Patir Alex brushed off his cassock and followed Theo to the ancient libation table, which clearly served as the center of activity.

Theo shared his worldly possessions: the icon of the Virgin, the portrait of his mother, the bundle of letters. The priest, visibly moved, glanced around him and started babbling about his fear of bats. Then he pointed to the shadow puppet made of worn leather that was leaning against Soc's haversack.

Theo gently snapped his finger against the leather as if to awaken Karagiozis from sleep. The puppet lurched to life. "Hey, Karagiozis, little old fellow, I would like you to meet Patir Alex," Theo said.

"Ah, Karagiozis," the priest exclaimed.

"Karagiozis Karagiozopoulos at your service, Patir," the puppet answered.

"Which story would you like me to perform, Patir? Karagiozis the Soldier? Karagiozis the Shoemaker? Karagiozis the Winebibber? A loaf of bread will bring you an unforgettable performance. Half a loaf? A quarter of a loaf? A few beans?"

Without waiting for the priest's reply, Theo said, "Ah, of course, Karagiozis the Soldier." Adopting a coarse twang, Theo made the puppet say, "I have the makings of a soldier, Patir. I will kill every kraut I see. I will become the bravest and fiercest hero that Greece has ever known." After a calculated pause, the puppet added, "But not this minute, Father. First I must tend to my cat, who is about to have kittens."

Patir Alex laughed until he shook, his laughter echoing in the cave chamber.

The priest surveyed the cave's nooks and crannies, his voice reverberating in the tomblike chamber. The only untenable aspect of life in this underworld was the bats. Theo saw the priest shudder, but Theo, too, was afraid of bats that inhabited the cave. But they both knew that bats were a source of food.

When Theo expressed a wish to serve as the priest's acolyte, Patir Alex kissed him on one cheek and then the other to signal his approval. "I swear on my brother's memory to avenge his death. I will fight to the end for the freedom of my country," Theo said. Patir Alex did not doubt him for a minute.

Into the priest's hands, Theo placed Soc's haversack containing the maps, copper wires, and other invaluable items.

"Karagiozis is just a wobbly old trickster at heart, always working at being a hero," Theo said.

"We will see about heroism," Patir Alex said, as they made their way back to the village. "A bit later on, not now," he chuckled.

⊙ ⊙ ⊙

Patir Alex's visit to the cave served as a catalyst for action. Theo, Fotis, and the priest carted icons, church implements, holy vestments to the cave. They also transported the printing press, all remaining weapons, and the village library of fifty books.

As Theo lifted the books into sacks, his fingers traced the ribbed spine of each one, the engraved gold letters meticulously crafted and decorated. At the top and bottom of the spine was the classic key design, and above the design on some of the books the priest's initials, AH (Alexandros Haralambos). A few books were roughly paperbound, tattered from use, among them Karl Marx's *Das Kapital*.

The village school resumed with Patir Alex as teacher and Theo, Fotis, and five other children as students. Even though the writings of the philosopher Plato had been banned, Patir Alex read aloud excerpts from his works—his description of Socrates' view of virtue, his view of the just person and the just society.

He read aloud from Plato's *Republic*. "Until governments are ruled by philosopher-kings, the world will not become a better place," Patir Alex said.

"*Gnôthi s'auton,* know thyself," the priest said repeatedly. "The philosopher Socrates, the ugly old badger with the bulbous nose, exhorted people to ferret out the truth beneath appearances, especially behind one's own face in the mirror."

☉ ☉ ☉

Although the Germans had issued an order banning all newspapers, Patir Alex, Kyria Maria, and the children made good use of a printing press that had parachuted from the skies, a gift from Allied forces. The Germans said that distributing leaflets was a crime against the state, punishable by death, but Kyria Maria was determined to communicate the latest news of the war.

Theo scrutinized each part as it was taken out of the two compact fiber boxes. About six centimeters deep, the X-Press came complete with paper plates, a grease pencil, ink, and directions for use.

Kyria Maria crouched over her radio system, earphones plugged firmly into her ears. At times amidst the crackling and static, she heard the voice of the British prime minister Winston Churchill. During the broadcast, she scribbled words on paper, words as painful and fiery as the burst of a rifle.

"Every act of retaliation emboldens the forces of the Greek resistance," wrote Kyria Maria. "*Aera*," she wrote, calling out the rallying cry of the mountain fighters. "*Zito eleftheria*. Long live freedom. *Zito* Hellas. Long live Greece.

"Axis forces crush human beings like grapes in the wine trough, *thrum thrum thrum* to the mournful tympanum of war.

"Stand bold, my people. We were not vanquished by the Italians, and we shall not be vanquished by the Bulgarians or by the Germans."

Theo was drawn into the work. "The Greek villager must sleep with his eyes open like the honeybee," Theo wrote.

"May your eyes be fourteen," he wrote, quoting the wise woman. "May they be twenty-eight."

The children delivered the pages, slipped them under the doors of villagers. Theo was especially cautious as he approached the home of the president of the village council.

"Athens high school student killed by krauts," began Theo's tribute to his brother. "Socrates Alexandros was executed for tampering with a store of olive oil in possession of the enemy. He was a youth of great courage who planned to become a doctor." Theo drew a thick black border around the death notice.

In the newspaper, Theo placed a small announcement about his upcoming puppet show. He also designed posters featuring a bold illustration of Karagiozis and placed them around the village.

Papageno and the president of the village council stood before one of the posters. Recognizing the familiar Karagiozis figure, Papageno leapt for joy and ran down the street, holding Mozart and singing the puppet's name over and over again. The president of the village council headed toward the office of the German commandant.

 THIRTEEN

From the open shutters of the priest's dwelling, Theo could see the mountains in the distance. The songs of the wise woman filled the house. She sang of memory and eternity and the immense brevity of life. "Life is a blade of grass," she said. "Life is a fleeting shadow."

The songs filled Theo with longing for something he felt to the core of his being but couldn't put into words. This longing overtook him sometimes in the church, the cemetery, the fields. But no matter what the circumstances, it was a call of the spirit, sweet and low and haunting.

Wanting something, yet not quite able to name it, Theo found an old piece of cardboard and carefully drew the figure of Alexander the Great, the Macedonian king who conquered the ancient world. On Alexander's head he outlined a war helmet crowned by an ornamental crest. He cut the figure out, repeating over and over, "Alexander lives and reigns." Then he cut out small openings in the figure, which he covered with thin paper to create a translucent effect.

Theo recalled that every time his godfather performed one of the Alexander stories, the audience cheered. He practiced the legend he was re-creating in his mind.

On a stormy, windswept night, a gorgon—a creature half fish, half human—rose out of the sea, grabbed on to the mainsail of a caïque, and at the pitch of her breath said, "Where is Alexander the Great?" In an earsplitting tone, the captain trumpeted, "Alexander the Great lives and reigns!" Sometimes he added, "And keeps the world at peace!"

When the captain answered that Alexander was alive and well, the gorgon disappeared, the rough sea became like oil, and the captain continued safely on his way. But if the captain gave the wrong answer, the sea simmered and churned, and the caïque plunged to the ocean bottom.

Theo worked slowly, painstakingly engrossed in his labor. Bent over Alexander like a scholar over a book, he chewed his lip. He shook his hair out of his eyes. He worked cautiously. He remembered how much Soc loved the legend. He drew the gorgon and the boat. With leftover cardboard he drew a Nazi tank and several Gestapo officers.

Theo turned toward Karagiozis. "Alexander lives and reigns," he made the puppet say. "He'll knock the goose-steppers off one by one."

Theo was distracted by the chirping of the bird he was nurturing back to health. "I will pay Petros back for the chicken. Don't worry," he said to the bird.

Daily Theo walked to his cave refuge. He crept through the tunnel to the room where he kept the gun. He looked at the markings, the date of manufacture, the shape. Beneath the toggle grip he observed the tiny engraved *P.08*. Above the chamber, the date *1940*. The handle was textured to provide a better grip.

Theo dismantled the gun. He unscrewed the barrel from the receiver. He separated the thin ejector and rear connector pin. He wiped each small part with a cloth until every iota of dust was off. He then put it all back together as if it were a small, challenging puzzle.

◎ ◎ ◎

As the weeks passed, Theo proved his usefulness to Patir Alex and Kyria Maria. He assisted with garden chores. He grew physically stronger every day and was able to carry water from the well without stopping to rest.

In the early evening, Theo performed plays for the priest and his wife. Patir Alex joined Theo on his hands and knees behind the sheet. Theo was surprised by his agility. In the plays about Greek history, the message was clear. Karagiozis's ancestors had paid dearly for freedom. He must do the same, for there was nothing more valuable, more real than liberty.

Late at night the three of them crowded around the wireless. The removal of one small screw enabled Kyria Maria to contact comrades in Operation Elijah. She deciphered the words, "Despite acts of enemy retaliation, the Greek spirit of resistance grows stronger. Archbishop Constantinos angrily protests threats and human-rights violations against Greek Jews living in Athens."

The contact continued, "The Nazis seem determined to wipe out the Jewish population of Athens."

⊙ ⊙ ⊙

One morning en route to the cemetery, Theo heard what sounded like a duet coming from beyond Papageno's rock cleft. At times Theo thought he heard more than two voices. He also heard the sound of an instrument, like a panpipe.

The striking beauty of the voices caused Theo to pause and listen. As his curiosity grew, he followed the sound and positioned himself behind a tree. He saw a youthful German soldier arm in arm with Papageno.

The soldier's war paraphernalia was thrown with abandon on the ground: a helmet, binoculars, a semiautomatic carbine rifle. Theo's eyes became riveted on the rifle. But he already had a weapon. How many weapons did one person need? he wondered. What would Soc make of this?

Theo could have snatched up the rifle and run for it, but he was frozen by the magnificence of the singing and by the Nazi soldier's complete indifference to danger.

"I'd give my finest feather to find a pretty wife," sang Papageno buoyantly. "And happily then ever after, we'd frolic in gladness and laughter!"

The soldier played various roles in turn. At first, Tamino, the Egyptian prince, and then Pamina, the beautiful princess with whom Tamino falls in love. "A man who feels the pangs of love, he will not lack a gentle heart," he sang. Sweet voiced and strong, the soldier's tone and demeanor were captivating. The beauty of the music filled Theo's heart, but his mind flashed to the cave and the gun.

 FOURT∑∑N

While Theo watched Patir Alex celebrate the exaltation of the cross in Vasilaki, David Elias listened to his rabbi father sing the *kol nidre* in Athens. It was Yom Kippur, the Day of Atonement, and the hottest Yom Kippur on record. Though it was October, Athens had been attacked by a raging swarm of mosquitoes.

The rabbi's forefathers had an unbroken lineage back to Greek antiquity. His father had been one of the founders of the Athens synagogue of Etz Hayyim. From hours bending over the holy books, Rabbi Elias had a stoop in his shoulders and the look of a scribe.

The only time Rabbi Elias displeased his parents was when he married Sophia Stavrakis, a Greek Christian. His first daughter, Sarah, did not change their perception, nor his second daughter, Rebecca, nor his third daughter, Elizabeth. When Elias's fourth child, David, was born, Reuben Elias was forgiven. The long line of rabbis would continue.

In the raging heat of an autumn day, as Rabbi Elias made his way to the temple, he was stopped by a German officer and handed the summons that he had been expecting. He was asked to appear before the head of the Rosenberg Commando. He glanced at his wristwatch. It was 3:30 P.M. The archbishop would be taking his daily siesta.

The rabbi swatted a mosquito that had landed on his arm. He wiped away the residue of blood with his handkerchief. With the same handkerchief, he wiped the sweat that had accumulated on his brow.

At 4:00 P.M. the rabbi telephoned the archbishop and then made his way to commando headquarters, where he was ordered to hand over the names, addresses, and professions of all Jews living in Athens. In addition, he was asked for a list of people who had assisted Jews. Rabbi Elias left in a high state of anxiety and placed a second call to the Greek Orthodox primate.

The archbishop's reaction was quick and bold. He went to the headquarters of the occupation command. "What have these Greeks done?" he inquired of the German officials. "What dastardly crime have they committed? Who is your God?" he asked.

The high-pitched whining of a mosquito around his head was annoying the archbishop. He followed the flight of the insect with his eyes and swatted it furiously on the desk that separated him from the Germans. They jumped back, startled.

In a subsequent meeting with the authorities, the archbishop again confronted German officials. He protested threats to the Jews and violations of human rights and human dignity. Nonetheless, the Nazi commander demanded information.

The archbishop and the rabbi considered the matter, and eventually the priest produced sheets of paper for the German officer. He exclaimed, "I possess a list of names that would be extremely valuable to you—people you could annihilate without the world suffering unduly."

The chief German official snatched the list from the clergyman's hands. The first name was the archbishop's own. It was followed by the names of every member of the Greek Orthodox clergy. The German official laughed at the list and muttered something about not wanting to be accused of persecuting the Greek Orthodox Church.

The priest and the rabbi were relieved that only a week earlier resistance fighters had broken into the Jewish temple and confiscated and destroyed the records of the Jewish community. In the once-bustling city of Salonika, tens of thousands of Greek Jews had been sent to death camps. The Salonika pogrom would not be repeated in Athens.

⊙ ⊙ ⊙

The archbishop arranged for fake baptismal papers for Rabbi Elias and his family. The chief of police issued new identity cards. Greek Christian friends hid Rabbi Elias's wife and daughters in their homes. The rabbi was aware of Operation Elijah's plans to alter his appearance by shaving his beard, dyeing his hair, changing his dress.

Rabbi Elias paid one final visit to the temple. He stood with David at the altar. The holy book open, the rabbi mumbled in Hebrew what seemed to be a prayer, but the more closely David listened, the more he realized that his father was talking to him.

"God will forgive us, my son, but we must mark this Day of Atonement as the day of your coming of age." David had been preparing for his bar mitzvah. It was scheduled for spring, at the time of his thirteenth birthday, when he would become a man and assume manly responsibilities. David gulped. But he understood the significance of his father's decision.

David haltingly read from the Torah and recited its blessings with only occasional assistance from his father. "You have been a good son and I have been proud to call you my son. From now on I will call you my brother," Rabbi Elias said. "May you walk in the ways of God."

FIFTEEN

Patir Alex and Theo left the village before dawn. Their destination was the Convent of the Virgin, where Andonis, the Gypsy, was scheduled to meet them.

A crescent moon, a thin sliver of silver, lingered above the horizon. The road was rough, unforgiving. Through the centuries, the sun had emblazoned itself on mountains and fields. It made the earth hard like brick and the riverbeds dry as cadavers.

Theo swung the saddle sacks over one of the mules. One was heavy with artillery, holy vestments, a silver chalice, and Communion wine. The other held a censer and cheese and bread for the journey. A shovel and pickax were tucked into the saddle.

The priest and the boy prepared themselves quietly, stopping only at the well to splash their faces and to fill their goatskin pouches. The sacred icon of the Virgin was wrapped in cloth and carefully placed in a sack that Theo carried like a bulletproof vest. Kyria Maria had pinned to the boy's trousers a clove of garlic to ward off the evil eye. In the sack the boy also carried his puppet.

Over one shoulder the priest wore a cartridge belt full of ammunition. Two cats scampered across the yard, their eyes lighting up the darkness.

As they urged their mules forward, they turned their heads in the direction of the wise woman's benediction, "Bless you, my children. May your eyes be fourteen. May they be twenty-eight. May they be as many as the stars in the heavens." The wise woman gave the priest a small bag of dried noodles. "These are for Andonis," she said.

The only person stirring was the golden-voiced Papageno, who sat cross-legged in his rock cleft. The strings of his crude lyre were sheep guts, his bow a stick with horsehair strung across it.

"Find your way to my house, Papageno," the priest called out, "while the wheat porridge is steaming."

"Thankyouthankyouthankyou, Patir. Karagiozis-KaragiozisKaragiozis," Papageno said, lumbering upward.

As the sun filled the horizon with the color of

ripe pomegranate, crags and fissures in the ancient crust were visible, scars formed by fracturing and mending. Rays of light gave prominence to gorges of breathtaking beauty—escarpments, long and precipitous, gaping ravines.

The travelers stopped at a small shrine to rekindle the votive light. At the threshold to the village and in places throughout the countryside, miniature whitewashed chapels dotted the landscape, each containing an icon and a votive light.

"At these sanctuaries," Patir Alex said, "some people make the sign of the cross because of devout religious conviction. Others make it to ward off evil spirits lurking at crossroads and in fields. Still others make the sign of the cross as a reminder that to bow down before the gods—to humble oneself before them—is wiser than to imagine oneself a god."

Theo and Patir Alex passed the vineyards and fields lying fallow. One farmer standing on his harrow led a team of two emaciated oxen, who struggled to pull a steel plow. It was the time of autumn sowing.

"Look, Patir, high in the sky, a hawk chasing wild pigeons," said Theo.

"The pigeons are no match for the hawk," said the priest.

"When will the war end, Patir?"

"When the hawk stops chasing pigeons, my son."

As the October sun rose in the sky, it became a flaming ball of fire.

"Have you ever killed a man, Patir?" asked Theo. As the words were uttered from Theo's lips, his mule lost its footing, fell backward, and then righted itself. Patir Alex didn't answer, and in a moment Theo could see why. The priest was distracted.

In the distance they could make out the outline of a man hanging by a parachute from the branch of a tree. The man's arms were pinned down hard against the branch, his head thrust forward and down on his chest.

Patir Alex quickly took charge and directed Theo, who hoisted himself up the trunk and cut the cords. The man dropped, and Theo could see that it was not the fall from the airplane that had killed him but a bullet through his chest. Blood was still oozing from a corner of his mouth.

He had a bushy head of hair, a cleft chin. The expression on his face, a half grimace and half smile, revealed a dimple. But now he was cold, colder than well water and still as marble.

On the arm of his jacket, he wore a British flag,

and pinned to the inside of his shirt was a gold heart-shaped locket containing the photo of a young woman. On a chain around his neck his dog tag identified him as Brian Kelly and gave his serial number, blood type, and religion.

The priest told Theo what they must do. He handed him the shovel from the mule's pack, and the boy began to dig into the hard, unyielding earth. Theo felt sweat forming on his brow and rolling down his face. He could feel blisters surface on his palms. His throat was parched from thirst.

Thoughts of Soc flooded Theo's mind. The youth was so like his brother. He gently unloosed the dog tag around the soldier's neck and put it in his pocket for safekeeping. And then Theo began to shake and tremble, not knowing whether from exhaustion, or rage, or fear.

Theo had dug no more than a shallow grave when he heard what sounded to him like a child's cry. He paused, looked at the lips of the dead soldier. He listened and then began shoveling again. The priest closed the paratrooper's eyes, wiped the dirt and blood from his face, and used a piece of the parachute as a shroud.

Theo tied two short branches together to form a cross. He collected a pile of stones and placed the cross securely in them. He leaned the icon of the Virgin against the cross and lit the incense while the priest said prayers for the soldier, his deep voice echoing across the hills, "Kyrie eleison. Lord, have mercy."

The black cassock of the priest was covered with dust as he called out, "May Brian Kelly's memory be eternal." Theo echoed, "May his memory be eternal . . . "

When the prayers were done, Theo went on, "Did you hear whimpering, Patir?"

"No," said the priest.

They folded the remaining parachute and packed it, strings and all.

In the shade of a sprawling plane tree, Theo unwrapped bread and cheese and surveyed the area.

The past was alive in the present. Spirits inhabited the mountains and fields. They lived in trees, in wells, in rivers, and in Theo's mind.

As he drifted into a half sleep, thoughts of the gun entered his mind. Theo shook himself awake again and looked toward the bandoleer of the snoring priest. Cautiously Theo edged toward it. He took three bullets and stuffed them in his pocket without so much as a yammer from the sleeping priest.

Suddenly from behind a tree a young girl appeared in a whirl of dust. She carried one child on her back, and one child clung to her side. Startled, Theo jumped to his feet. He quickly spit three times and uttered an incantation against evil spirits. "Honey and milk in your path, honey and milk, honey and milk."

The girl seemed to be Theo's age. One child, a boy, seemed no more than four years old. The smaller boy, a toddler, was perhaps two. Theo worried that one of them had seen him take the bullets.

Theo nudged Patir Alex awake. "Ah, that I had honey and milk," the girl said. Her eyes were thimblefuls of turquoise sea. At Patir Alex's gesture of approval, Theo reached into the sack for bread and goat cheese and handed the loaf to the girl.

"Thank you, oh, thank you very much," she said. "Bless your hands," she added, as she divided the bread and gave pieces to her brothers. They all pounced on the food.

In one hand, the younger brother clutched to his chest a purse that emitted a rank odor. He did not want to part with the purse, and only after the coaxing of the priest did he let go. It contained the remains of his kitten.

"It is Patir Alex's job to bury the dead," Theo said. "Your kitten is on the road to God," he added reassuringly.

The child blinked, but he did not protest as the priest performed a short burial service.

The girl told how she and her brothers had returned from the fields to find their home razed to the ground. She called out to her parents, but they were nowhere in sight. She searched the vicinity of the house, but they had disappeared.

"How far have you walked?" Theo asked.

"There are twelve nights between my village and here," she answered. If Theo's calculations were correct the children had walked at least a hundred kilometers. "Zoe," she said, introducing herself. "My brothers, Plato and Achilles. Our parents are Lilika and Stavros Zevgos from the village of Skala."

☉ ☉ ☉

Patir Alex's job became more dangerous with the addition of the children. The priest reasoned that his growing army would serve as church vicars, acolytes, gravediggers.

They executed their job well. In the next fifteen

kilometers, the priest and the children buried a mule and three Greek partisans killed by machine-gun fire. But the work was exhausting, so the travelers gave up digging and began covering bodies with stones. They marked their progress with a trail of burial mounds.

By evening they arrived exhausted at the Convent of the Virgin.

 SIXTEEN

The Convent of the Virgin, like the nest of an egret, was perched high on the brow of a hill. The convent housed sixteen nuns—*kalogrias*—as well as the miraculous icon of the Virgin. The holy image was enveloped in gold and silver ex-votos. Made from thin sheets of metal, the items symbolized afflicted body parts—arms, legs, eyes. Villagers had brought them to the convent with an appeal to the Virgin for help.

On this October night, Abbess Eugenia was not alarmed by the pealing of the entrance bell. She was accustomed to interruptions by German officers as well as by her own people.

Yet when she opened the door, the reverend mother was relieved to see Patir Alex and a bevy of children. "Many children, much luck," she said, warmly embracing the priest. The exhausted travelers were given dippers of sweet water from the well situated in the center of the courtyard.

Adjacent to the main building, Theo noticed a chapel dedicated to a beatified eighteenth-century hermit, the Blessed Simeon. A flagged marble pathway led through a sequestered garden with majestic trees and, beyond that, an arched entranceway to the courtyard.

When she observed the children's bedraggled condition, the reverend mother sighed. Zoe and her siblings were caked with dirt, and their clothes were ragged and torn. They were covered with scratches and had bruised elbows and knees. The little boys' cheeks were like dried-up riverbeds from their tears. The reverend mother whisked Zoe and her brothers down the hallway for warm baths and food.

A young monk inhabited the small domicile attached to Blessed Simeon's chapel. He performed the services that the Greek Orthodox women were forbidden by church law to perform, including daily matins, vespers, and other sacred duties.

With the monk, Theo explored the labyrinth of corridors and winding pathways and underground cellars. He could feel himself relaxing in the security and peace of the place. The monk told him that a poet had once stayed at the convent as a guest seeking rest and restoration. But this was before the war, when the convent had many such visitors. Now its visitors were fugitive Jews and wounded soldiers—Anzacs, Brits, Scotsmen—en route to safer territory.

Mother Eugenia's spiritual idealism meshed perfectly with an abundance of opportunity in her tiny enclave. Under her watchful eyes, the Convent of the Virgin had become transformed into a clandestine hospital, a repository for several of Greece's most cherished antiquities, and a major locus in the network of underground tracks used to save Greek Jews and other fugitives from Hitler's Third Reich.

Patir Alex settled in the convent library, where the abbess brought out *masticha,* a licorice liqueur, and a cache of filbert nuts. They toasted their good fortune at meeting once again. Theo joined them.

It wasn't long before Andonis arrived. Theo admired the Gypsy leader's rugged good looks, his full beard, black bushy eyebrows, and coarse black hair down to his shoulders. Theo was distracted by the tassels on the poppy red bandanna tied around the Gypsy's head. What a nice detail to ornament a puppet with! Theo thought.

Patir Alex and Andonis grinned with old affection. They had known each other from childhood. At least twice a year Andonis's father had visited

Vasilaki with an organ-grinding machine and performing monkeys. As a small boy, Patir Alex had wandered away from the village. He was found by Andonis's Gypsy *kumpania,* or caravan, where he spent several days.

As the priest and the Gypsy leader drank to each other's health, Patir Alex commented to Theo that he measured life as before Andonis and after Andonis. The Gypsy leader's help had greatly increased Patir Alex's effectiveness in the resistance movement. The storage bin under Andonis's wagon served as a transport for fugitives and arms.

"*Zito* Hellas," Andonis said, clinking his glass against Patir Alex's.

"*Zito,*" rejoined the priest, bringing the brandy to his lips.

"*Zito,*" said Abbess Eugenia.

Theo listened as the three exchanged news, information, rumors. In some ways Patir Alex and Andonis were very much alike, both capable of quiet generosity and courage.

As food was being warmed, Theo turned in Andonis's direction. The Gypsy leader told Patir Alex and Abbess Eugenia his mounting fears about the fate of Europe's Gypsies. Andonis's voice became a whisper. "They are classifying Gypsies as well as Jews." He handed Patir Alex a piece of paper on which was written the German system of classifying Gypsies. Theo scurried to peer over the priest's shoulder.

Z	*Zigeuner,* full Gypsy
ZM+	*Zigeuner Mischling,* predominantly Gypsy
ZM	*Zigeuner Mischling,* with equal Gypsy and German blood shares
ZM-	*Zigeuner Mischling,* predominantly non-Gypsy
NZ	*Nich Zigeuner,* free of Gypsy blood

Theo caught Andonis's eyes. They were black as berries and penetrating. Andonis continued, "The Nazis are even arresting people merely for looking like Gypsies. And I hear that German Gypsies are being forced to wear the letter *Z* just as the Jews are forced to wear the letter *J.*"

"You don't think the bear trainer's death . . . " the priest asked.

"No, not here. Not yet. They are too busy rounding up Jews," said Andonis. "No. I think the Germans are hungry. The bear had meat on its ribs."

"But it is not only the enemy that surprises me.

It's the betrayal among our own," said the priest. "The president of the Vasilaki village council commandeers a black market, charging exorbitant prices for cigarettes, flour, sugar. And, as if this was not enough, he plays backgammon with the German commandant."

"Even as a boy, the president had no soul," Andonis answered, shaking his head from side to side.

"Tomorrow," Patir Alex said, "we head back to our village. Comrade, our plan is clear, yes? Unless you hear otherwise, in two weeks to the day, we will meet once again here at the Convent of the Virgin. God willing, I will have the rabbi and his son at my side."

"May the hours be blessed," Andonis said.

With his last spoonful of egg-lemon soup, Andonis called out in a gravelly voice. "Gather round, little ones. I have a story to tell," he said. "It's called 'Yannakis the Fearless,' about an orphan boy who does not understand the meaning of the word *fear*." Eager to increase his repertoire of Karagiozis plays, Theo leaned closer to the storyteller.

Andonis told the story with gusto.

"Once upon a time a young man named Yannakis left his village to go in search of fear. He packed his possessions in a kerchief, threw them over his shoulder, and bid his sister, Clio, good-bye. 'I beg you, Yannakis. Don't go,' Clio cried. 'There are too many dangers lurking in the world.' Tears fell down her cheeks, but Yannakis, ignorant of fear and curious about its meaning, started on his way.

"After traveling for several days, he came to a river wider than the wingspread of Zeus's eagle. Yannakis couldn't see the opposite bank nor even a finger's length into the river's murky depths. To get to the other side, he boarded a ferry boat and noticed passengers surveying the rough currents and talking anxiously about a mermaid who demanded a human sacrifice to ensure the boat's safe passage.

"Waves thrashed against the stern, threatening the entire vessel. 'What should we do?' asked a vegetable farmer with baskets overflowing with chickpeas, courgettes, and squash. A chicken farmer tried to quell his clucking hens to keep attention from himself.

"An old man, bent like a broken tree, said, 'I'll go. I can barely see and my bones are all brittle.'

"Moved by the old man's courage, Yannakis said, 'No, Grandfather. You have stories to tell.' He tied his bundle of goods to his belt, and, fully clothed, he dove into the river. Yannakis was not at all afraid that he might never again see the light of day.

"While keeping himself afloat with one hand, he grabbed the wicked mermaid with the other. Holding on to her luxuriant raven hair, he demanded, 'Why are you threatening these innocent people?'

"The mermaid, stunned by his daring, fell in love with Yannakis and took him to her cave, where she kissed him and gave him a sack of priceless golden curiosities. 'Take anything you want—all of it, if you would,' she said, but Yannakis took only one glittering bracelet for his sister, whom he missed very much.

"One amazing adventure followed another in which Yannakis's ignorance of fear caused him to be rewarded with untold wealth.

"Finally, longing for home, Yannakis returned to the village with a sizable fortune, but he confessed, 'Dearest sister, I encountered nothing to make me afraid.'

"His kind sister shook her head. They hugged each other and celebrated his return. On his first night back, Yannakis excused himself and walked outside among the trees to answer nature's bidding.

"In the dark of this moonless night, while he was squatting and grunting and still wondering why his sister was afraid of the dark, a stately stork with a long sharp beak approached silently, stealthily.

"No sooner had the stork's beak snapped on his fleshy backside than Yannakis clattered loudly and flapped his arms. 'Dear sister,' Yannakis yelped, shaking in his boots and struggling to pull up his trousers, 'I'm afraid.'"

Andonis's audience roared with laughter.

"From that moment forward," Andonis said, "Yannakis and Clio lived peacefully and happily for the rest of their lives."

Theo asked Zoe if she knew the meaning of the word *fear*. "Yes, I do," she said, "but I also know the meaning of the word *bravery*. It is possible to know two things at once." Theo wondered if he would know fear and bravery together, both at the same time.

The following morning, Andonis placed the arms and artillery under his wagon and carried them away.

 SEVENTEEN

Theo watched the wise woman decode the message. An airdrop was scheduled on the night of the new moon. Theo and Patir Alex devised screens of saplings to protect their small circle of signal fires from being identified by the enemy. Then they settled in to wait.

Theo fidgeted. In his head he worked out details of a "Yannakis the Fearless" show. He chewed on a finger. The night was silent except for his own breathing and the shrilling of cicadas. Waiting is by far the hardest thing in war, thought Theo.

Although there was no moon, Theo fixed on a throbbing red star in the eastern sky. He had just about given up hope that the plane would arrive when he was jolted to life by a tawny owl that darted across his line of vision like a specter in the darkness. And then he heard the drone of an engine.

The hum grew louder as the aircraft dipped its nose toward the light and dropped its cargo. As the pilot pulled upward, he swept the plane's silver wings sharply to the left, then to the right in a spirited greeting. "*Zito* Hellas," Theo whispered, as he waved his arms and saluted the pilot.

Theo and Patir Alex had no trouble finding the parachutes. Patir Alex cut the parachute cords from the packages, and Theo folded the chutes. They dragged the packages toward the village and into the church, where they stored them in the inner sanctuary.

The following night, with the help of Kyria Maria and the children, they carried the packages to the cave. "This will be useful." Kyria Maria's eyes sparkled as she touched the silk material. She was anxious to transform the chutes into shirts, sheets, and pajamas for the convent's hospital and for the mountain fighters. The rigging lines would become thread to knit stockings.

Patir Alex cautiously unwrapped each package as Theo and the others looked on. In one package, there were tins of bully beef and small amounts of sugar, flour, and cigarettes. In another, flasks of rum. In another, Sten guns, grenades, tiny bars in cellophane wrappers, gelignite explosives. Patir

Alex scrutinized each article. He smelled it, listened to it, and, if he deemed it safe, passed it on so that the curious children could hold each thing.

And then great hoots and howls from everyone when one package revealed chocolate. They celebrated the success of the mission by slicing the chocolate bar evenly. "Hey, how about me?" Theo made Karagiozis exclaim. "I am hungry. My children are hungry." When he thought no one was looking, one of Zoe's brothers popped the extra piece into his mouth. Patir Alex rewarded himself with a British cigarette and a swig of rum.

That evening they watched as Theo performed a puppet show of Yannakis, the boy who went in search of fear. Theo used some of Zoe's words to end the story: "It's possible to know fear and bravery at the same time." Patir Alex raised his eyebrows, but everyone else clapped.

For the first time in weeks, Kyria Maria made bread from stone wheat flour. She used a paddle to mix the flour, water, sugar, salt, and dry yeast. She kneaded the dough, shaped it into a round loaf, and even though it was nighttime, she baked it in the stone oven behind her house.

The scent of freshly baked bread filled the house. When he awakened, Theo saw the plumpest loaf of bread he had seen since before the war. It was an enormous mound shaped like the dome of a chapel. In his mind he cut a piece for Soc, a piece for his parents, a piece for the puppeteer, a piece for his cat. "May your hands be blessed," he said to Kyria Maria.

◉ ◉ ◉

Their next mission posed a greater challenge—blowing up a train. Theo and Patir Alex were members of a team charged with placing bundles of explosives under the rails. Wires connected each bundle, and the ends of the wires were inserted into a detonator. When the wheels of the engine made contact with the detonator, the explosives would go off, blowing up the train.

On the surface there seemed nothing complicated about the assignment. But there was a German post in the vicinity of the tracks. The slightest provocation alarmed the Germans and they shot recklessly.

It seemed to Theo that there were Germans everywhere. On either side of a nearby bridge, guards in their stations held an almost perfect view over the landscape. Each station had a powerful searchlight and an arsenal of machine guns.

Patir Alex earmarked the railway track switch, one of the weakest points along the line, as their primary target. Theo ran in a crouched position, his arms and hands almost touching the ground. Patir Alex followed some five meters behind. Both carried knapsacks filled with explosives.

It was midnight, and a cool wind at last refreshed the air. Theo waited for Patir Alex at the railroad bed adjacent to the switch. He hunkered himself like a bush at the side of the tracks and waited, praying that Patir Alex was fast on his heels. Theo licked his lips. He bit the loose skin on his upper lip.

The searchlight beam scanned the tracks within centimeters of Theo's position. He broke into a cold sweat. Bravery and fear, he intoned, with all the intensity of a monk at his prayers.

He waited. It seemed an eternity, but in reality it was no more than minutes before the priest, breathing heavily, reached him. Almost without pause, Theo and Patir Alex placed charges of explosives between the rail and the switch, and then on either side of the track, at intervals of two meters. Again the searchlight made its round. Theo made sure that the detonator wires were securely attached, and then he and Patir Alex scrambled back a safe distance and waited.

Clickety-clack, clickety-clack. The rattle of the train on the tracks. Instantly alert, Theo huddled and prayed. Seconds seemed like hours, but suddenly a flash like lightning ripped apart the night sky. Metal piled on metal, smoke on smoke, and fire rose from the pyre, the great crawling beast hissing and spitting. One car slammed into another amidst flashes of lightning and the crack of thunder. The sound ricocheted off the mountains.

At the first sound, Theo felt satisfaction. Until he heard the screams of wounded soldiers, the hysteria.

My God, thought Theo. For a moment he was torn between running toward the disaster to offer help and prayer and retreating toward the village. His heart was filled with fear and confusion from the noise, the chaos of blood and darkness. No beauty in heroism. Only cruelty. Theo clapped his hands over his ears as they ran toward the village.

Unbeknownst to the guerrillas, the lead car of the train had carried sixty Greek hostages, as a deterrent to saboteurs. More then two hundred Germans were severely wounded, almost one hundred were killed. All sixty Greek hostages died.

When they heard the news, Patir Alex and Theo clung to each other and sobbed.

 EIGHTEEN

"In any act of sabotage," Patir Alex said, "timing is essential." He turned to Theo and the other children. "Do you recall the myth about the three women who possessed only one eye between them? Danger occurred when the eye was being handed by one of them to the other. For that split second the three of them were totally blind."

"A split second of vulnerability," Kyria Maria said.

"The instant to strike like a serpent," Patir Alex added.

Theo's eyes grew larger as he listened to the priest and the wise woman.

The priest continued. "The guerrilla action in the village of Koliva is a case in point. The plan called for the villagers to welcome the German military convoy as it passed through en route to their garrison. To offer the soldiers food and drink. In fact, to get them good and drunk.

"And then, from the hills like jackals the guerrillas pounced on them, suddenly, viciously."

Kyria Maria sighed. "I worry about growing acts of German retaliation: fifteen villagers arrested and shot for an attack on a military car, ten others executed for harboring a British paratrooper.

"These young olive shoots," she added, "no taller than rifles, called upon to be heroes."

Theo quickly interjected, "A hero avenges the death of his loved ones. A hero destroys trains and disrupts communications. A hero is fearless."

"Only sometimes," Patir Alex said. "I've seen heroes—you will pardon me, children—piss in their pants in fear."

Turning to Patir Alex, Kyria Maria said, "Really, Alex, must you be so candid with the children? They are frightened enough as it is."

"Truth is an ally, Maria, always an ally. You need to hear this, Maria," Patir Alex added. "The Germans are corralling Gypsies as well as Jews into death camps. Andonis has heard of major pogroms against his people."

"What does it all mean, Alex?" Kyria Maria asked.

"It's hard to know," Patir Alex responded. "When we are young," he continued, "we must learn to walk twice, once when we lift ourselves from all fours and master the art of walking upright. Someone—mother, father, aunt, uncle—reaches outstretched arms toward us, coaxing us on our way.

"But we must learn to walk a second time, when we are a little older, this time in the shoes of another person. This, too, is risk taking and must be nurtured by someone who has mastered the art, someone who reaches toward us, beckoning us forward. This is a hard knowledge: that very little separates one person from another person. This knowledge is both a burden and a responsibility.

"The difference between our humble Theo and Greece's crown prince is merely a matter of circumstance, and the difference between them is not deserved. Theo would make a goodly king," Patir Alex said.

"The difference between Adolf Hitler and me," Patir Alex added, "is that although I can imagine what it is like to be evil, Herr Hitler cannot even for a second imagine what it is like to be good. Those who know the good, choose the good."

Patir Alex shrugged his shoulders. "Enough philosophizing," he said. "Fortunately, I am a village priest, and Theo and I are mountain fighters about to embark on a feast for our brothers. The meeting is tomorrow night, and we have yet to provide the celebratory lamb. To enter the sheepfold, a fox about Theo's size is required—no more." Theo's heart started beating rapidly.

"How much danger is there, Alex? The boy already has been asked to risk a great deal."

"If we can maintain our steadfastness, our calm, our composure—if we can control our bladders—there will be no risk. What do you think, Theo? Do you have the makings of a hero?"

Theo held up his Karagiozis, and in the coarse twang of the puppet, he said, "Oh, yes, I have the makings, but you will excuse me, Patir. First"— Theo hesitated for a moment, not wanting to be misunderstood—"I must water the tomatoes." Patir Alex laughed. Theo put the puppet down and said, "When do we begin?"

The priest reached into the bowl of his mandolin and unfolded the map on the table and a drawing of the sheepfold. The slender-necked mandolin had been sitting idly in need of repair. "I have targeted a weak spot and have loosened the soil under the barbed-wire fence at this point," he said, pointing to the drawing.

"The German sentry spends most of the night dozing. Here the famous German instinct for efficiency collapses. The sentry is usually fast asleep by 2:00 A.M. as the Dipper makes its way toward the horizon. This is the moment of vulnerability we must seize."

Patir Alex went over the plan again and again until Theo knew it by heart. He would creep toward the sheepfold, scoop out the loosened soil, and crawl through the opening.

In the quiet of his room, Theo confided to Karagiozis. "What if I freeze in place and am unable to move?" he whispered to his puppet. "What if I sneeze? What if the lamb is too frisky? What if the soldier wakes up?" Theo could feel a rifle butt against his body.

"Are you brave or a quivering excuse for bravery?" Karagiozis prodded.

Theo asked Zoe to take care of the copy of Soc's letter to Barba that he had been carrying. She handed him her kerchief. "It will bring you luck," she said.

☉ ☉ ☉

A clinking of bells signaled that Patir Alex and Theo were approaching their destination. In the distance they could hear the faint chorus. The sound had come less frequently since the beginning of the war.

Patir Alex pointed his gun with its silencer directly at the sleeping soldier. He motioned Theo forward.

Cautiously Theo crept toward the sheepfold. He scooped out the dirt and stole under the barbed wire. He stuffed dried grasses into the bell worn around the animal's neck, silencing the clapper. He tied shut the lamb's mouth with Zoe's kerchief and tied his two forelegs together and then his two back legs. Theo lifted the lamb in his hands, first scrambling under the wire himself and then pulling the lamb out.

It was not until they had returned to the house that anyone noticed the long gash made by the barbed wire on Theo's arm.

Impressed by Theo's stealth, the priest began to call him Little Fox. Theo swaggered and preened like a rooster.

"No quivering excuse for a hero here," he called out to Karagiozis.

 NINETEEN

The remarkable efficiency of the kill. One cut of the knife and in ten seconds the animal becomes unconscious. In thirty seconds the animal is dead. The bleating cry of the sheep ceases. Red blood oozes from lips, ears, mouth onto the white fleece. The animal quickly stiffens and becomes cold and lifeless.

Theo observed the shepherd in charge of butchering the lamb. Before the war, he had herded three hundred ewes, rams, and goats, but when the Nazis confiscated his flock, he joined the resistance. In preparation for the mountain fighters' feast, the shepherd inserted a stick in the lamb's back leg and rapidly moved it up and down to loosen the flesh from the skin. He blew into the hole and the animal became inflated like a balloon. He slapped it a few times to loosen the skin, which he then pulled off. With a swift motion of the knife, he sliced the animal from its tail to its throat and pulled the intestines free; then he removed everything else. The entire animal was edible.

The mountain fighters roasted the lamb over an open fire and sipped the clear wine flavored with resin. When the lamb was cooked, each man devoured a portion of the meat with a huge chunk of bread. They toasted their good fortune. "Bravo, Theo," they called out, whacking him on the back and filling his wineglass.

The men had not allowed themselves this much wine in a long time, and they became tipsy with exhaustion, exhilaration, and alcohol. The shepherd scraped the shoulder blade clean and held it up to the light. The lines and shapes formed a pattern on the translucent bone, and the shepherd became a fortune teller. Against the chirruping of cicadas, he cheered his band with predictions of good news.

Theo couldn't keep his eyes off the rebel leader. He had seen a poster of the man, a profile, with the word WANTED written in bold letters on the top. Theo had imagined a very different face from the one that was in front of him.

In order to rule the guerrillas, the leader had to exhibit iron strength and ruthlessness. But in person the fierceness alternated with disarming warmth. His most striking feature was his riveting silver blue eyes.

Theo was aware of the rumors about the guerrilla leader. It was said that he possessed an explosive temper and was capable of great violence, that once he killed someone for stealing a few eggs. Probably more than anything else, it was the air of unpredictability that struck fear in the hearts of his followers. They likened him to the volatile *meltemi,* the wind that appeared as if from nowhere with its own peculiar rhythm, at times uprooting everything in its path.

No one who had seen it could possibly forget the sight of the "black bonnets," the *kapetan* and twenty-five of his men, the lead corps of the resistance, riding hard in black sheepskin hats on the strongest, blackest, healthiest horses.

Theo listened as the men talked about revolution, economic equality, and the disappearance of class distinctions. He heard the names Marx, Lenin, and Engels bandied about. The men argued about the good life. They railed against Benito Mussolini's Fascism and Adolf Hitler's Nazism. They railed against the king.

The only thing they did not rail against was

Communism. Most, like Patir Alex, supported a form of internal Communism, an abolition of the monarchy and private property. They believed in ending economic exploitation.

In the midst of lively chatter as the men picked over scraps, the voice of the rebel leader bellowed, "Enough of talk! Politics is action! Bring out the prisoner!"

Prisoner? thought Theo, who was not very used to wine and wondered if he had misheard. His blood ran cold. What prisoner?

Theo watched as a youth was driven in front of the men like a calf to slaughter. The men had taken his shoes and his coat, leaving him barefoot in rolled-up trousers and an undershirt. They goaded him forward as if he were a sow to market. One of them swung his sickle over the prisoner's head in a mock beheading. Another hit him hard with a long stick.

"Let the child kill him," one of them cried out. Startled by the command, Theo bowed his head, drifted back in the pack. Was it the *kapetan* who had called to him? Had this not been what he had been waiting for, dreaming of?

The eyes of the men focused on him. "Yes, yes, let's bring the boy to manhood." The leader placed a sicklelike blade in Theo's hand and loudly coaxed him forward. "Strike, strike!" he cried.

Notions of revenge, retribution flashed in Theo's head, but the young man in front of him seemed like a wounded bird and not much more than a child himself. His hair was the color of ripe corn, his eyes pleading and disconsolate. He held his hands together tensely as if in prayer.

Theo glanced at the men. Their eyes were red from sleeplessness, their lips parched, chins full of stubble. They were gripped by madness, their voices frenzied. He glanced at the prisoner, now naked except for a blindfold. He was on his knees and shivering.

For an instant, Theo glimpsed Soc in the prisoner and became embarrassed and overwhelmed by self-consciousness. The meaning of Patir Alex's words rang in his head. *The difference between himself and the prisoner was not deserved.* Theo threw the blade down and cried, "*OXI*. No." He raced into the woods, leaving the men stunned.

Theo perched himself nearby and watched, tear-filled, wondering if somehow he had just betrayed Soc. The band of men remained silent. The man closest to the prisoner handed him his shirt.

⊙ ⊙ ⊙

Theo couldn't bring himself to speak to Patir Alex about the incident. Patir Alex said only a few words to the boy. "What I witnessed," he said to him, "was the summit of bravery."

 TW∑NTY

Theo was startled awake. David! And Rabbi Elias! Standing wearily in the doorway, they had arrived from Athens at last, worn out from days of upheaval and the wrenching act of separating from their family.

Theo leapt from his sleeping pallet and embraced David, who smiled faintly and almost fell from exhaustion.

"We were given fake documents," Rabbi Elias said, "including baptismal certificates and identification papers, but oh, everyone has muttered their direst predictions that I, as a public figure, might be recognized."

Theo listened attentively as Patir Alex reviewed the route. "Rest, eat, regain your strength. But listen as you do. Past the threshing floor, the barren fields, north northwest, in the direction of the North Star," he instructed, pointing to the map. "Andonis will meet us at the Convent of the Virgin and travel with you to the coast, where you will be met by fishermen who will take you by boat to Smyrna.

"Rabbi Elias, you will become Patir Elias. Dressed in one of my cassocks, who will know the difference?" The priest chuckled. The rabbi did not chuckle in return. Theo noticed the rabbi's eyes. Only his eyes might betray him. Maybe because he had to leave his wife and daughters, his animated eyes had become cold.

"David will carry the icon of the Virgin," Kyria Maria said, as she gently awakened him. He had nodded off at the table almost before he could lift a cup of Kyria Maria's good broth to his lips. She helped to strap the icon to his breast. "The Virgin will keep you awake." Kyria Maria packed a small amount of cheese and hardtack biscuits for the journey. She also placed a small jar with a firmly sealed lid. "The jar is for convent Communion wine," she told Theo. "Abbess Eugenia is expecting it.

"Kyrie eleison," she said.

As they left, Theo saw Rabbi Elias turn to the wise woman: "Thank you for what you are doing. It will not be forgotten."

Theo stood near David. He helped his friend

adjust to the pack animal. "Are you all right?" Theo asked him. "Karagiozis and I miss you."

"Thank you," David responded. "Since we last met, I have been bar mitzvahed. It was a quiet, informal event, just Dad and me. Nonetheless, you are now, ahem, looking at a man." He grinned playfully. "Have you become a hero yet?"

Theo chortled. "I've decided to stick to puppets," he said. Theo wanted to tell David about Soc, but he couldn't get the words out and decided to hold the news for another time.

The rabbi and his son and Patir Alex and Theo had traveled no more than fifty meters when a figure darted toward them, calling out the priest's name. Theo recognized the familiar face of a farmer from a neighboring village. "You are urgently needed, Patir, to administer last rites."

The priest assured Rabbi Elias. "Theo will see you on your way. He knows the route as well as he knows his name." He embraced his companions and then he left with the farmer.

They had gone only a short distance when Theo heard a commotion approaching from ahead of them. It was too late to move out of sight. A jeep rattled around the bend directly toward them, flying a black swastika against a scarlet field flag. It was followed by tanks a few moments later.

A German rolled out of the leading vehicle, dusted himself off, straightened his jacket, and confronted Rabbi Elias. Theo recognized the officer as the German whom villagers called Schnapps because of the strong smell of liquor on his breath.

"Where are you going?" he slurred.

The rabbi answered quickly, "To the neighboring village. The sacraments of the church go on, with or without war."

The soldier's eyes fastened on the boys. He walked slowly around David, eyeing him, and poked at his shirt. The whites of his eyes were yellow and his fingers were stained with nicotine.

David stood still, expressionless. Stay calm, Theo whispered to him in his mind.

"What are you hiding?" the Nazi said, grabbing at the boy's shirt. David did not answer. The soldier pulled at the buttons tearing the garment open and stared for a few uncomfortable seconds into the eyes of the Virgin. He turned abruptly and got back into his car.

As they pulled away, Rabbi Elias made the sign of the cross as a gesture of respect for the god of his Greek Orthodox brothers.

"Yes, you are on our side, dear Virgin Mary," Rabbi Elias said, a twinkle returning to his eyes.

Theo and David grinned at each other. The close call unleashed a well of emotion.

"Where will you go in the New World, David?" Theo asked.

"To New York," David answered.

"We will meet again," Theo said. "God willing, I will go there, too, one day."

Theo and David chattered about the rare and excellent lives they would have in the New World, avoiding the good-bye they would soon have to say. They would go to the same school, join the same teams. They would go to Yankee Stadium and cheer on the Yanks. And Theo would attend Friday night services with his friend, for by that time certainly the whole Elias family would have arrived safely in America.

Only Soc will not be there, Theo thought, still unable to say the words aloud. Instead, he said, "Please visit Barba." He scribbled on a piece of paper Barba's address in Sunnyside, Queens. "Write to me from America. Tell me exactly where you are. I want to know every detail about your life. And scout out a place for my puppet theater."

Theo was unable to say the word *good-bye*. It

was too painful a word, evoking another loss, still raw and smarting. The boys held on to each other until Andonis arrived exactly on schedule and motioned David into the Gypsy caravan and camouflaged him with layers of canvas as if he were a bale of straw.

 TWENTY-ONE

As Theo entered the coffeehouse, one villager was making an aggressive assault against another in the climax of a three-hour game of chess. The room was square. Several wooden tables were covered with cracking oilcloth. The drab gray walls of the coffeehouse were totally bare except for a large photograph, touched up with paint, of the liberal political leader Eleftherios Venizelos.

The portrait revealed the man's broad forehead, balding pate, and white hair and beard. His eyes were sparkling behind rimmed spectacles.

Stacks of old newspapers, yellow and tattered, were piled high on a low wooden stool. Pericles, the proprietor, subscribed to two newspapers, one representing the voice of the far left and the other only slightly less liberal. Both papers were on the side of Eleftherios Venizelos in protesting the return of the king to Greece.

Through tobacco smoke that shifted and came together in strange configurations, Theo counted twenty-five rickety wooden chairs. He estimated the room could hold at least ten more. Good.

The proprietor owned a small Victrola on which he played music. Could Theo use that, too?

Theo took the proprietor aside. "We may need more chairs," Theo said. "We have sold a lot of tickets."

"Delighted," Pericles responded. "There are at least ten more in the back of the store."

"Would it be okay if I set the stage up here?" Theo said, pointing to the space in front of Venizelos's portrait. "You will take a cut of the profits, of course, and you will make considerable money from drinks of patrons." It was the best business arrangement Pericles had made in months.

◎ ◎ ◎

In preparation for the puppet show, Theo rehearsed every day, Zoe at his side. In addition to serving as an arsenal and refuge, the cave became a puppet workshop. Theo worked hard at getting the puppets ready, making sure that there was enough mobility in the joints, that the rods were in place and could be securely attached, that scenery and props were completed.

Theo worked diligently over props. He made several swords, two bouquets of flowers, a watering can, signposts, cannons. He sanded *soustas,* the wooden sticks that would be attached to the puppets. He also made swastikas, Greek flags, banners, standards, Stukas—the ugly German dive-bombers—and puppets representing Benito Mussolini and Adolf Hitler.

He practiced his newly created Benito–Herr Hitler show, adding a dramatic segment about the much-longed-for fall of Il Duce. Theo taught his troupe riddles to warm up the crowd. He made Karagiozis ask, "What has a neck but no head?

"What? Nobody knows?" Karagiozis teased. "A bottle," he answered.

Zoe interrupted, "Do you know the greatest fear of partisans during the revolution against Turkish oppressors?" Her voice was suddenly serious. "Their greatest fear . . . " She hesitated for a moment and then she blurted out, "Their greatest fear was having their heads lopped off by Turks as they lay on the battlefield dead or dying."

"That's not funny," Karagiozis said.

"But it's true. Wounded soldiers begged fellow

soldiers to cut off their heads and take them with them. They feared defilement by the enemy."

"Well, Nazis aren't Turks," Theo said. Then he crooned:

"The mountains are snow-covered,
The springs have dried up,
The mills grind no more,
What was long has become short,
And the two have become three."

When the children seemed stumped, he answered, "Old age."

"Another!" clamored the young ones.

"It is white, it is not cheese,
It is not a bulb of garlic, or an onion;
Nobility and the poor use it;
On the table it is not put."

"Soap," chirped Zoe. "My turn," she said.

"He is not a king,
He wears a crown,
He has no watch,
He counts the hours."

"A cock," Theo called out. "How about this one?" he continued.

> "A thousand knots, a thousand holes,
> A thousand guesses, and doubtful if you find it."

Again the children were stumped.
"A net," Theo exclaimed.

☉ ☉ ☉

Theo squeaked on a cornet, and Zoe beat the bottom of one of Kyria Maria's kettles in what amounted to an overture to the show—a prelude to the appearance of the hero Karagiozis. Cymbals rang as Zoe's brother stood like a small *evzone*, a member of the honor guard, clanging on signal.

The children often doubled over with laughter, slapping each other on the back, fighting over roles. Theo attended to the arrangements.

Theo took shifts with Zoe and the others selling tickets at the coffeehouse. In return for the best seat in the house, the town crier agreed to announce the show in the village square.

"Let's make a pact that we will be friends forever," Theo said to Zoe, "that no matter how separated we become, we will remember each other, and that no matter in how much trouble, we will help each other."

"And that no matter how hungry, we will share our last crust of bread," Zoe said.

"Like bees," Theo said, "we will share food with each other until not a crumb is left."

"So then, let's call our pact the Pact of the Sword Bearers," said Zoe. "But how shall we seal it?"

"With words," Theo said, "and the sign of the cross. I solemnly swear that if I have to, I will chop your heads off, little ones," he added, turning to Zoe's brothers, "and yours, Zoe, rather than allow the enemy to take them," he said.

"I solemnly swear that I will chop Karagiozis's head off rather than allow the enemy to take possession of it," Zoe said, making the sign of the cross. "And yours, too, Theo."

Theo began to giggle and the four of them suddenly erupted into howls of laughter.

 TW≷NTY-TWO⊙

A few old men grumbled about the use of the coffeehouse as a theater for shadow puppets, but Pericles geared up for a profitable evening. If it was a success, he agreed he would give Theo a chicken. Success would be measured by the number of espressos he sold, the number of ouzos, the drachmas he made on refreshments.

The house was sold out. People came in droves.

Theo wrangled Papageno into singing *"Der Vogelfänger bin ich ja"* (The Bird Catcher Am I) as the audience arrived. "There is no rarer bird than I. I'm always happy, ho hi hi; the songbird catcher all does know, yes, young and old where e'er I go. For I can lay a skillful snare, and with my piping drive out care . . . "

"Hear ye, hear ye, hear ye," trumpeted Karagiozis. "Presenting Benito the Buffoon and his sidekick, Herr Hitler."

Theo was standing behind the puppet screen. With a long wooden stick, he brought Benito the Braggadocio against the white cloth. The audience could see only the shadow of the puppet. Theo had created a surprising likeness of Benito Mussolini, capturing Il Duce's jutting jaw and bald head. He threw the puppet's chest forward in an exaggerated manner and held the puppet's head back so that his chin protruded.

He brought Benito's hands to his hips, his legs astride. Benito strutted back and forth, back and forth, boasting of *otto milioni di baionette*—eight million bayonets.

He adapted Benito's habit of gesticulating only with his right hand. On-stage he placed Benito on the balcony of his home, the Palazzo Venezia. Theo knew that Benito was a violinist, so he attached a violin to his other hand.

He had also created a puppet of Adolf Hitler: his pomaded hair parted decisively on the right, his high forehead, fulsome nose, small mustache. Theo called the puppet Herr Hitler.

Theo and Zoe brought Benito and Herr Hitler onto the swastika-draped stage together. At first the two men spoke very softly, pianissimo. They were terribly polite, exchanged niceties, and puffed each other up with flattery. But then Herr Hitler's voice became fortissimo.

"Dolt, idiot!" Herr Hitler screamed at Benito. Herr Hitler was dressed in knee boots and breeches. "I like you, Benito, I admire you, but you are stepping on my corns. Can you believe that anyone in his right mind ever called me Germany's Mussolini? What an insult!" His voice was furioso.

"You, Herr Hitler," retorted Benito, "are a comic clown, a bully, a scared rabbit with quivering paws."

Theo had devised a way of opening and closing the puppet's hand, in imitation of Hitler's clenched fist. He alternated that movement with outstretched arms, forefinger stretched toward heaven. In one hand he attached an ox-hide whip. Theo thrust out the puppet's arm in a Nazi salute.

"Did you know," Herr Hitler said, "that I can hold my arm like this for hours, that I have an arm of granite?"

"Did you know, Herr Hitler," said Benito, "that I am undefeated in fencing? Will you accept my challenge?"

The two dictators strutted back and forth with exaggerated posturing and chortles from the audience, who pelted them with catcalls and acorns.

○ ○ ○

When Theo and Zoe brought Alexander the Great and the seven-headed dragon on-stage, the audience was in an uproar. Each time Karagiozis lopped off one of the dragon's heads, people rose and cheered.

"One head—Hitler," called Karagiozis. "Chop. One head—Benito Mussolini. Chop. One head—Bulgaria. Chop. One head—hunger. Chop. One head—poverty. Chop. One head—cruelty. Chop. One head—war. Chop." As Alexander defeated the seven-headed dragon, Karagiozis shouted out, "Better one hour of freedom than years of slavery!"

Onto the stage trotted a Gestapo puppet holding the German swastika. Karagiozis raced over to him, thrashed him on the head, ripped the flag from his hands, and simulated tearing it into shreds. As he did so, Zoe threw the already prepared pieces into the air. On signal, every puppet in the repertoire walked onto the stage, each puppet waving the blue-and-white flag of Greece. Every villager in the audience stood up and began singing the Greek national anthem.

It was then that three shots rang out and utter

chaos reigned in the coffeehouse. The portrait of Eleftherios Venizelos fell from the wall and shattered into pieces. Chairs and tables were overturned. Bottles and glasses crashed to the floor. Someone sent the Victrola needle screeching across a record. Theo and his crew dove behind the puppet screen and held on to each other.

The Nazi aim was to disperse the crowd—to panic the Greeks and send them running for their lives—and they achieved this quickly and efficiently.

⊙ ⊙ ⊙

A story circulated the following day that Saint Zacharias's bones would one day chase the Nazi soldiers clear over the nearest cliff and the president of the village council into the small crawlspace under his house.

Pericles made good on his bargain. With the chicken in hand, Theo went to repay Petros, as Soc had told him he must.

 TWENTY-THREE

As the weeks went on, German acts of brutality escalated. "The enemy calculatedly destroyed hundreds of beehives, golden and thriving in the noonday sun," Kyria Maria wrote. "The ghosts of myriad dead hummed and swarmed and flapped their wings in psalms of grief. All are lost, *Lelé, Lelé*."

Patir Alex and Kyria Maria did not expect the severity of the reprisals. The Monastery of Constantine and Helen was desecrated. Its treasures were plundered, its monks thrown over the cliff's edge to their deaths.

The village of Katharo Nero: seventy dead.

The village of Mikro Papoutsi: fifty-seven men killed by machine-gun bullets.

The village of Daktilos: seventy people executed.

The village of Kato Elaia: forty-six executed.

"In a battle near the village of Vasilaki," Theo

wrote in his notebook, "Greek mountain fighters killed fifteen German soldiers. There are rumors that the Germans will seek quick retaliation."

⊙ ⊙ ⊙

During all of the violence, the president of the village council hid in his home behind closed shutters.

Patir Alex, Kyria Maria, and Theo went about their business discreetly and effectively until one morning, in the rose light of dawn, German soldiers shattered the door of Patir Alex's home with an ax.

The noise jolted Theo to his feet. He awakened Zoe and her brothers and gathered them close to him.

The priest had barely scrambled out of bed when a Nazi officer kicked him to the floor with the tough tip of his boot.

Patir Alex and Kyria Maria had rehearsed this scene again and again. They would say nothing to provoke the Nazis. They would stand tall like the great plane trees of the village. Yet, when it happened, they were unprepared and surprised.

In a quavering tone, Kyria Maria's voice rang out, "The Lord is my light and my salvation, whom shall I fear? The Lord is the strength of my life, of whom shall I be afraid?" An officer spit in her face. Kyria Maria wiped the saliva off her cheek with the back of her hand.

Theo watched from the next room. He saw blood streaming from Patir Alex's mouth, and he heard the wise woman's voice. He bolted toward Patir Alex only to be swatted back by one of the soldiers.

"Though a host should encamp against me, my heart shall not fear," Kyria Maria continued. "Though war should rise against me . . . "

The screaming and fluttering of Theo's bird distracted the officer. He picked it up and threw it ruthlessly against the wall. Theo winced as he heard the thud of the bird against the hard surface and saw it drop to the floor, its feathers all distorted, its breast puffing weirdly.

Theo blinked his eyes, expecting the world to explode inside his head. Kyria Maria looked in his direction, motioning him toward the open window with her eyes. Suddenly he knew he must move.

He signaled the children toward the window. They slipped out in their night clothes and stumbled over roots and tree trunks as they ran toward the cave. Only seconds spared Theo and the others.

The young ones, in tears, bedraggled and

frightened, needed to be coaxed forward. "Come, precious ones, we're almost safe," urged Zoe.

Once safely in the cave, Theo wasted no time. He crawled into the small room where he kept the gun and with shaking hands loaded it with three bullets.

"May God be with you, Sword Bearer," Zoe said.

Crows cawed in the wind as Theo raced back toward the village. He tried to embolden himself by repeating the name Patir Alex had given him. Little Fox, Little Fox, he said over and over as he ran silently, his only trace the writing of feet on the ground. He took no notice of the softly breaking dawn. In the village there was no sign of Patir Alex. All soldiers but one were gone. Only one. The air was still.

Theo peered through the window and saw Kyria Maria tied to a chair at the mercy of the German officer. Her hands were tied roughly with a coarse cord behind her back; her hair was disheveled; her cheek bore the bruised imprint of a hard slap. On the floor next to the chair lay the inert body of his bird. Kyria Maria's eyes were fluttering, betraying terror.

"Where is the printing press?" the soldier circled the chair, his rifle pointed at her heart. "We know it's in the village. Where, vermin, scum, sow?" He was impatient and furious at her silence.

"We know a great deal about your clandestine

activities," he ranted. "You and your rebel priest will pay for the train debacle, among other things!" chortled the officer. Theo saw the flash of his match as he lit a cigarette and inhaled deeply.

Kyria Maria's lips began trembling and the officer snapped, "What did you say?" He baited her. "Where? Where are the Jews? Speak louder. Louder!" Kyria Maria kept repeating the words of Psalm 27.

Act, Theo said to himself. Quickly, before it is too late. But he was frozen, unable to move.

The officer scowled. He moved toward her with his cigarette. He singed her hair.

Theo's anxiety turned to terror. Pull the trigger, for the sake of the Virgin, he said to himself. "Shoot the gun, little fellow," he heard Karagiozis urging him. "Now. Now."

The soldier again moved toward Kyria Maria.

Theo held the gun in both trembling hands. He forced down waves of nausea that filled his gut. Every muscle in his body was taut. He aimed at the soldier, and petrified, he pulled the trigger. The startled man lurched forward, reached out his arms for support, and then dropped to the floor at Kyria Maria's feet.

Theo raced inside, untied Kyria Maria's hands,

and held her shaking body in his arms. He brushed her hair back with his hand, whispering over and over again, "It's okay now, *Manamou,* mother of mine. It's okay."

Theo reached down and lifted a floorboard and took the wireless in his hands. He took the icon of the Virgin from the alcove and wrapped his bird in a fold of paper. Kyria Maria grabbed the priest's mandolin and without looking back they made their way to the cave.

◉ ◉ ◉

A messenger brought news that Patir Alex had been hanged by the neck until dead on the hill called Golgotha. "To the very end," he said, "he recited Psalm 27. The Germans refuse to let anyone approach his body," he added, "or the bodies of the two others hanged with him. They have burned homes in the village, also the coffeehouse, the school, the church. Nothing was spared."

The messenger hesitated and then continued, "On the third day, the Nazis unloosed the cord around Patir Alex's neck, but they still refused to give up his body. They let it lie there unburied in a heap—carrion for vultures."

Kyria Maria burst into tears, and sorrow occupied the cave, drifting around corners, through narrow passageways, and over the libation table.

Cruel, cruel Nazis. Theo wept. Did they have no honor, no decency? The image of burial mounds filled Theo's mind. Stones carried and laid one on top of the other. Stones piled high into mounds. Stones commemorating the final rite of passage. "Patir Alex, Patir Alex," he called out. His chest ached and his head was bursting. He knew what he must do.

On a shard of pottery, Theo meticulously inscribed the letters *OXI*. Under the word, he inscribed *I.X.N.K.* (*Isous Christos Nika*, Jesus Christ conquers). He tied together two pieces of wood to make a cross.

In the depth of night, with Kyria Maria's blessings and prayers, Theo stole out of the cave toward Golgotha, the site of the execution. He negotiated his way forward through a wilderness of stones and rocks, his stubborn will struggling against forces far larger than himself. The thought of seeing the motionless body of Patir Alex filled him with fear. Patir Alex, dead? He blanched at the idea. The word *dead* coursed through his body like a bolt of electricity.

Theo crawled toward the heap on the ground

that he recognized as Patir Alex. He rested his head on Patir Alex's breast as if listening for a miracle. He placed Patir Alex's arms on his chest. He closed the priest's eyes. "Thank you, Patir Alex," he said. "I will never forget you."

Theo was overtaken by a sudden numbing drowsiness. His eyelids became heavy, and for a second he longed to fall asleep next to his old friend, but he pushed himself onward.

He placed the small hand-hewn cross in the priest's hands. From his own pocket, he took the gold coin that Rabbi Elias had given him as he left Athens. "This is to assure your safe journey," he whispered.

Theo placed the coin in the priest's mouth and put the shard of pottery on his lips. He scooped up a handful of earth and sprinkled it on his body. "*Eonia, e mnemne,* May his memory be eternal," he chanted. Lifting himself slowly from his knees, he made the sign of the cross and, crouching, backed slowly and respectfully away from the scene.

As he reached the outskirts of the village, Theo stopped at the threshing floor, a circle of ground marked by a low wall of stones where the grain was separated from the straw. Farmers had located it on high ground to catch the wind and made it ring-shaped to ensure a circling path for the yoked oxen as they dragged the threshing sledge over the wheat.

Only the wind whipped in wild abundance over the wasted floor, blowing Theo's tawny hair as he looked at the abandoned sledge, now rusted and unused, and surveyed the landscape. He broke off a piece of the sledge to use as a shovel.

Theo had imagined the winds fanning and whipping flames, transforming Vasilaki into ruins. But when he saw the ravaged village in the distance, he shuddered at the spectacle, fell to his knees, and uttered a long, low moan, like the mournful echoing sound of wind and thunder. The view filled the once-green garden of his heart with unpalpable losses. The spasm of grief lasted a few moments or hours; he was not sure because he woke either from sleep or from a swoon—and caught the scent of smoke from the rubble in the distance still smoldering.

☉ ☉ ☉

In the chaos of the Nazi pillaging and terror, Theo's Karagiozis had become lost. Theo set for himself the task of finding the puppet. He searched for Karagiozis in the ashes of Kyria

Maria's house, the church, the coffeehouse. Theo's small frame was doubled over like a little old man bent by age. The implement in his hand resembled a walking stick. Theo scrutinized every inch of earth. With the piece of broken sledge, he lifted layers of ash and debris. He uncovered a cooking pot, broken roof tiles, charred picture frames.

He lifted his head toward the smoke-scarred, blistered entranceway to the church. As he went inside, he looked at the damaged wall frescoes. Only the wings of an angel were visible. The gold-gilded book in the evangelist's hands and the face of the Virgin were darkened by smoke. He uttered a prayer for Patir Alex.

Theo was gladdened to see Mozart's skull on the altar. His eyes scanned the church for Papageno, and he found him hunched in a corner, whimpering, covered with ashes and soot. "Papageno," Theo whispered, kneeling by his side so as not to frighten him. "Papageno, Papageno, thank God you are alive."

"KaragiozisKaragiozisKaragiozis," Papageno said, relieved to recognize Theo. They sat with their arms around each other, comforting each other, until Papageno lumbered to his feet, picked up Mozart's skull, and blew some of the ash away.

Theo and Papageno made their way out of the church arm in arm.

On the ground near the house, Theo spotted something. His hand trembling, he reached over and lifted the object carefully. Karagiozis's head. Theo found an arm and a leg. "Poor sad, brave fellow," he said.

Theo celebrated his discovery. "I knew you'd show up, little fellow," he sighed.

Hours later, as he mended Karagiozis, he confessed to him, "Zoe is right, you know. Heroism is fear and bravery together, but it is something more. It's also knowing about good, about regret, even sadness at what one may be forced to do."

He brushed Karagiozis's cheek affectionately. "You know," he made the puppet say, "you are sounding more like that brother of yours every day." Theo chuckled. He thought of Soc and Patir Alex. Would they regard him as a fool? he wondered.

☉ ☉ ☉

In the countryside and village, the yattering of guns and the sudden crackle of an automatic eventually faded into the background. Hitler withdrew his troops. Slowly the tinkling of bells and bleating of flocks echoed over the mountainside, and the timpani of cicadas and strutting roosters regained authority.

In time, another kind of struggle reasserted itself—the determination of the villager to rebuild, to plow and harrow, to grind the corn and winnow the wheat, to sow broad beans, and to tend the vines and fruit-bearing trees.

Theo wrote to his uncle in America. He told him the tragic news. "Dear Barba," he wrote. "Kyria Maria needs me, and I must find my godfather. I have a sister now and two young brothers to look out for. And Saint Zacharias's bones. In time, I would like to attend the university, although I'm still thinking about becoming a master puppeteer. Would you look out for David Elias? Did he make it?"

Theo showed the letter to Kyria Maria. She read it thoughtfully. "When Prometheus took the gift of prophecy from the human race," Kyria Maria said, "he replaced it with the gift of hope. Your voice, Theo, is the voice of hope." Theo was touched by Kyria Maria's words.

⊙ ⊙ ⊙

Theo often held one of Patir Alex's books in his hands, following the priest's initials on the spine of the book with his forefinger. He wanted people to know that Soc and Patir Alex had meant every-thing to him. He felt that they lived on in him, that they were inscribed indelibly in his heart.

Theo's interest in the gun slowly faded, as his knowledge of healing and the power of words and language grew. The village threshing floor sur-vived the war, and the silver green olive and the lowly mallow also endured.

In Theo's heart small and large sorrows dwelled side by side, but light flooded the folds and sinews of his soul.

GLOSSARY

aera [ah-EH-rah]
Air, breath, freedom as opposed to oppression, a
rallying cry of the Greek people during World
War II. Also an acronym for Anglis/Ellas/Rossia/
Ameriki (England/Greece/Russia/America),
countries that were allies against the Germans.

eleftheria [eh-lef-ther-EE-ah]
Freedom, liberty.

Eonia, e mnemne [eh-aw-NEE-ah ee MNEEM-
nee]
May the deceased's memory be eternal.

Gnôthi s'auton [GNAW-thee sahf-TAWN]
Know thyself. Ancient Greek saying, credited to
Socrates, Greek philosopher 470–399 B.C.

Isous Christos Nika [ee-SOOS kree-STAWS nee-KAH]
Jesus Christ conquers.

Karagiozis [kah-rah-gee-AW-zees]
The name of Theo's puppet as well as the name of Greek shadow theater.

koulouria [koo-LOO-ree-ah]
Hard-crusted bread rings doused with sesame seeds, sold by street vendors.

Kyria [kee-REE-ah]
Mrs.; title of courtesy and respect for a married woman, used with a woman's first name as well as with her surname. Also means lady.

Kyrie eleison [KEE-ree-eh eh-LAY-ee-sawn]
Lord, have mercy.

"Manamou ta, Manamou ta klephtopoula" [MAH-nah-moo TAH, mah-NAH-moo TAH klef-TAW-poo-LAH]
"Mother, dear Mother, the klefts." First words of a popular kleftic ballad. Klefts (or brigands, rebels, guerrillas) were honored during the Greek War of Independence (1821–1827) as patriotic freedom fighters.

opa [AW-pah]
Leap, jump. In Greek folk dance, an exclamation of joy used to urge dancers on.

oxi [AW-hee]
No; one of the rallying cries of the Greeks.

pallikaria [pah-lee-KAH-ree-ah]
Brave ones; usually used to describe young men in the prime of life.

Patir [PAH-ter]
Father, title of respect and reverence for a priest.

xemetrima [ksee-MEE-tree-mah]
Incantations or ritualistic words to ward off evil and to break a spell.

Yiassou [YAH-soo]
Health to you; a popular greeting for hello and good-bye.

zito [ZEE-taw]
Long live, as in "Long live Greece!"

GREEK SHADOW THEATER

Just before World War II, Greek shadow theater was at the height of its popularity. High-spirited puppeteers traveled from village to village performing in outdoor cafés. The puppeteer created stories from current political events, history, and myth, and often used the dialect of the region in which he was performing. He sang ballads, poetry, and hymns about the War of Independence against the Turks, and brought to life the heroes of the Greek struggle (1821–1827). The roots of the Greek Karagiozis theater can be found in the Ottoman Empire; the roots of the Turkish shadow theater can be traced to the Far East. The word *karagoz* is Turkish and means black-eyed.

Every Greek recognizes Karagiozis as a trickster, a fool, a mischief maker, a comic hero, an everyman, everywoman. Although poor and downtrodden, the feisty little man is full of cunning and bravado and can finagle his way out of the most difficult situations. As theater of the people, beloved by children and adults, Greek shadow theater relies on the people for inspiration and affirmation.

Ta Klephtopoula

Ma - na - mou ta, Ma-na-mou ta kleph -to-pou - la,——

Tro - ne ke tra-gou-da-ne, o - lo pi-noun ke glen-da-ne.

2. Ma ena mikro, ena mikro klephtopoulo,
   Then troi, then tragoudai, ai, then pini, then glendai.

3. Mon t'armata, mon t'armata tou kitaze.
   Tou, dou fekiou tou lei, Yiassou, Kitso mou, leventi.

—Musical notation by Gilda Vretea Kornhauser

I.S. 61 Library

DATE DUE

FIC   Harrison, Barbara.
HAR
           Theo

BC# 3006100025218S $18.99

LEONARDO DAVINCI SCHOOL IS 61Q
           98 50 50TH Ave
    Corona   NY 11368

I.S. 61 Library